The Secret Diary of Mycroft Holmes

The Thoughts and Reminiscences of Sherlock Holmes's Elder Brother, 1880-1888

The Secret Diary of Mycroft Holmes

The Thoughts and Reminiscences of Sherlock Holmes's Elder Brother, 1880-1888

By S.F. Bennett

Belanger Books

The Secret Diary of Mycroft Holmes, the Thoughts and Reminiscences of Sherlock Holmes's Elder Brother, 1880-1888 © 2017 by S. F. Bennett

Print and Digital Editions© 2017 Belanger Books, LLC

ISBN-13: 978-1544140087

ISBN-10: 1544140088

For information contact Belanger Books, LLC

61 Theresa Ct.

Manchester, NH 03103

derrick@belangerbooks.com

www.belangerbooks.com

Book and Cover design by Brian Belanger

For Frances
from the
Western Wind

Introduction

In 1976, an innocuous bundle of journals went under the hammer at a provincial auction house in the south of England. Age-worn and stained with port and gravy, the pages of seemingly random numbers were thought to be of a mathematical nature, compiled by a student of calculus. The buyer had purchased them as waste paper with the intention of using them to stoke his fire. Fate intervened when he was converted to electricity and the journals were instead banished to the attic.

It was only ten years ago when the buyer's grandson recognised them as being an obscure code that their true meaning became clear. Someone had attempted to decode them at some time in the past, for pages with annotations in another hand accompanied the volumes. It has been speculated that it was Sherlock Holmes who had attempted this feat. Given the location where they were purchased, it is not beyond the bounds of reason to assume they found their way to the auction house from the remains of Mr Holmes's estate.

Now fully translated, the diaries have been one of the most exciting discoveries of recent years. Our understanding of Mycroft Holmes had hitherto been obscured by his brother's own reticence. Before the discovery of his writings, we knew little of this remarkable family's relations, because Sherlock Holmes told his biographer little. There was vague talk of his ancestors being country squires, but nothing of his immediate family. The revelation that Sherlock Holmes had a brother came only when necessity demanded it. Mycroft Holmes was more forthcoming in private, revealing that art in the blood does indeed take the strangest of forms.

Delicacy and the Official Secrets Act have rendered some details of his work for the government sealed for all time. But we are allowed a glimpse into his daily life: the meetings with ministers, dealings with staff, and the usual office mischief. A good deal of Mycroft Holmes's time was also spent fretting about his sibling's apparent lack of success or dealing with those minor inconveniences that came with being the brother of a consulting detective.

Whatever Mycroft Holmes's own feelings about his brother's profession, Sherlock Holmes does allow that his elder brother is his superior, stating that his powers of observation were superior to his. The diaries show this to be true, for there were several occasions where Mycroft Holmes proved himself an able, if sedentary, detective.

Further light is also thrown on that most intriguing establishment, the Diogenes Club. Like its founder, it was a unique institution. When the archives were destroyed by fire in 1933, after a stray spark ignited a pair of socks left by a member on the hearth in the library, it was feared that the history of the club was lost forever. We now learn that as a founder member, Mycroft Holmes was on the club's committee, which was responsible for every aspect of the institution, from repairs and renovation to finances and the election of new members. The diaries also offer insight into the structure, dynamics and staff, notably its nervous chef of questionable talent, the long-suffering hall porter, and the club secretary, tasked with daily administration.

Despite his best intentions, Mycroft Holmes was an irregular diarist, and entries have been selected on the basis of their interest pertaining either to his work or his dealings with his brother. Where necessary, footnotes have been added to facilitate the reader's understanding of the period.

It is hoped in making these diaries accessible to the public that Mycroft Holmes may at last be fairly represented. We have thus far been able to view him only through the eyes of his brother and Dr Watson. Now his thoughts and observations may speak for themselves.

S.F. Bennett
2016

Thursday, 1ˢᵗ January, 1880

There comes a time in every man's life when he must pause to take stock of his affairs. Whether one is taken at the flood or finds himself approaching the mid-point in his allotted three-score-years-and-ten at an alarming rate of knots, the realisation that one has been eking out an existence with precious little to show for it comes as something of a revelation.

The advent of my own epiphany in this respect came when the Honourable Francis Reginald Stoop announced that he had employed someone to write his memoirs. This is a man whose chief achievement to date is an ability to peel onions without crying. How he does it is the talk of the Foreign Office, and it has been said that it gave him an advantage over another candidate who could boast only hairy ears when it came to promotion.

That this qualifies him as a person of interest is something to which I take exception. When I questioned him about the

1

content of his endeavour, he tapped his nose and made some specious remark about 'having lived'.

If that were the only qualification, then the popular press would be awash with tales of people who 'have lived'. In my own case, that I have lived is evident, for I have the bills to prove it. When it comes to specifics, however, either my memory is deficient or I have been frittering away those years which the good Lord gave me with reckless abandonment.

I find that, should I be called to account for my time on this earth, I should have trouble explaining how I fill my days.

It is with this consideration that I have gone to the expense of purchasing a journal for the recording of those thoughts and events that disturb the otherwise humdrum pattern of one's life. That it has cost me a guinea. I consider a worthwhile investment. The shagreen cover is of excellent quality and the paper, so the stationer assured me, with a meaningful wink, will 'see me out'. I appreciate the guarantee, if not the sentiment.

On the question of my thoughts outliving me, it occurs that one day in the distant future, some enquiring soul may delve into these papers to learn of the daily life of a gentleman in the latter years of this toilsome nineteenth century of ours. If he is an enterprising fellow, he may even use the material to blackmail my heirs.

With that in mind, I have devised a code of my own invention to allow for the recording of my thoughts, secure in the knowledge that none of my peers shall ever probe the musings contained within these pages. What the family might make of them, however, is another matter, for I daresay, given enough time and motivation, even they, and one of them in particular, would eventually penetrate their depths.

Of course, I flatter myself in assuming that I shall find anything of interest to record. We can but try, as the saying goes, and I have no doubt that it shall prove most trying, especially at the end of a long day.

But if Samuel Pepys could fill nine years' worth of journals with tales of arguments with his wife, visits to the theatres, fire and plague, then I am fairly confident I should be able to achieve a similar feat – with the exception of the plague, that is. Wives too shall be avoided, excursions to theatrical events kept to an absolute minimum and fires confined to fireplaces and winter evenings. Other than that, I have resolved to record events and conversations exactly as they happened, for one never knows when one may need to account for one's whereabouts or provide evidence in cases of slander.

In this spirit, therefore, herewith commences the diary of Mycroft Holmes. I find myself to be aged thirty-three years, rising thirty-four this year.

How I got to be this old, heaven only knows, for I have had tribulations enough to debilitate the strongest of constitutions. My health is good, save for a touch of gout. My employment, facile though it may be, is tolerable, and my prospects for advancement, avoidable. Given that I can go no higher in my particular field, being at the apex already, I should say that any ambition in that respect would be wasted.

My comforts are few but welcome. Were I never to stir from my chair again, I could rest content knowing that I have contributed to the greater happiness of my fellow man. My chief achievement to date is in the creation of a gentlemen's club, The Diogenes, which caters for the unsociable man who wishes for the status and privilege of being a club member without having to endure the inconveniences of sociability. We have no club bores. In fact, we do not allow conversation at all. As one of the founder members, I made sure that this rule was written into the constitution.

If this résumé appears somewhat pedestrian, I counter with the consideration that it could be worse. One should always be grateful for one's lot, for it is certain that there are others less fortunate than oneself. It is also fair to say that there will be others better placed, but their cause is not mine. It is a rare fellow who can say he is happy with his life, and for the most part, I can say that I have arranged my affairs most adequately.

The only blot on this ordered horizon is that constant source of irritation and anxiety otherwise known as my younger brother, Sherlock.

I was told many years ago that to have a sibling was a blessing. There have been days, however, when it has felt more like a curse.

My charmed existence as a single child ended at the tender age of seven years. We were at Southsea in Hampshire at the time, visiting a decrepit relation of whom my dear father had expectations. On New Year's Day without fail, Great-Uncle Berengarius would issue a notice declaring that this year would be his last, and dutifully the family would assemble to pay their respects. Equally, every year, the gathering grew smaller, whittled away by natural wastage. In the event, Berengarius outlived them all. Such is the way of such things.

I had accompanied my father on this mission whilst my dear mother remained at our lodgings complaining of feeling delicate. At the time, Father had put it down to her over-consumption of candied fruit and pickled eggs of late, which he said was the cause of her becoming 'fleshier every day'.

Had I known how my life was to change, I should not have returned home that day but run off to sea. I say this, although I doubt I would have done so, even if the chance had presented itself. The sea is too quarrelsome for me. Given that I was once taken unwell in the bath, I daresay that a life on the ocean waves would not have suited me at all.

As to the day in question, I cannot say I was not warned. A crusty old fisherman on the pier had growled at me that 'storm-clouds were a-gathering'. Certainly, there was a thunderstorm soon after. One wonders if it was not prophetic, for we returned to find my dear mother had been delivered of a healthy baby boy, quite to everyone's surprise.

I cannot say that this was met with universal rejoicing. My father was of the opinion that, as head of the household, he felt he should have been informed if my mother had intended to make an addition to the family. To this, my mother replied that she had been meaning to tell him several months ago, but when the new fashions arrived, it had quite slipped her mind.

I can quite believe this, for she was the most delightfully absent-minded woman ever to don a bonnet. She lost herself once in Oxford Street; she was eventually found having a ride on an elephant at the Zoological Gardens. Names were wasted on her, for she invariably invented her own. Indeed, I attribute my own name to a misunderstanding at the font, either on her part or that of the vicar, for until her death, she steadfastly refused to call me anything but 'Merryweather'.

What she had actually intended for Sherlock, I would not care to speculate.

Something heroic and inspiring might have been advisable, for there is a want of purpose in my brother that borders on self-indulgence. In those of tender years, this can be forgiven, but, Sherlock, soon to be twenty-six in several days' time, can hardly be said to be a stripling youth. Maturing nicely, one might say. Into what, however, is debatable.

I say this because of his appearance at the club this evening. Come dusk, he appeared like an orphan of the storm with mud on his shoes and straw in his hair. I thought to impress him by enquiring as to what investigation had involved his disguising himself as a groom. It transpired that he had slipped on an icy patch in the street, soiling his clothes in the process. A closer inspection of the straw revealed a certain half-digested quality about it, and I suggested, tactfully, that he should make himself presentable. This is the Diogenes, after all. We do have a reputation to uphold, even in the Strangers' Room.

When he returned, the straw was gone, and over sherry, I ventured to ask him what his plans were for the year.

"Much the same as last year," said he.

To me, this meant another twelve months of idling.

"Having dithered for a quarter of a century," I said, "isn't it about time you found yourself decent employment?"

"I have employment," he countered.

"But is it *decent*, my dear boy?"

The nature of Sherlock's 'employment', as he describes it, has been a bone of contention between us since the day he announced he intended to forge his own path. To my mind, spending half the day lounging around in one's dressing gown does not constitute employment of any kind. I say this to him often, not to be unkind, but because I believe he is wasting his talents. I tolerated his abandoning his studies, on what seemed to be a whim, and have, as any dutiful brother would, supported his pursuits ever since. Quite what they are, I am at a loss to say. When I asked him once, he informed me that he was pursuing those 'avenues of investigation which may one day be useful to him in his trade'.

At the time, I thought this an appalling admission. Men have been expelled from their clubs for lesser indiscretions. Had our dear departed father ever heard him using that word, he would have dropped down dead from the shock.

As a general rule, the members of this family do not have 'trades'. We have debts, we have gout, occasionally we rouse ourselves and get married, but on no account do we dabble in 'trade'.

When I reiterated my thoughts on this point this evening, Sherlock had the gall to roll his eyes. He does this when he feels I am overstepping my authority. One day, to quote that sage of the Holmes family, Great-Aunt Dorothea, the wind will change and he will stay that way.

I further felt obliged to remind him that it would not be the first time someone was cut off with or without a shilling for dishonouring the family name.

To this he replied that it was impossible to dishonour the family name any more than our ancestors had done. In fact, so he said, by his reckoning, he had already improved upon our family history by finding an occupation that was not only *legitimate*, but did not involve cattle-rustling, coin clipping, poaching, or anything to do with racehorses.

I was most offended by this. I asked him what he thought of my working for the government. His answer to that was unprintable. I can only hope that he never expresses such an opinion before the Prime Minister. Hanging, drawing and quartering may have fallen out of fashion in this country, but I daresay the Prime Minister might be tempted to revive it on account of a provocative remark like that.

The evening ended, as usual, with our failing to reach any sort of agreement. The advent of a New Year has made no difference to us at all. Sherlock shall continue idling. I shall continue to divide my time between Whitehall and Pall Mall. At this rate, I anticipate that by this time next year we will both be older but none the wiser.

Worst of all, I detect a burgeoning sentimental streak in my wayward brother. He actually had the audacity to wish me 'Happy New Year' before he left. It was a good thing he chose that moment to leave or I should have had him excluded for such temerity. As it was, I was slow getting out of my chair and he was able to escape just retribution.

What I have done to deserve such impudence I do not know. My peers seem to have perfectly normal younger brothers. One is a gambler and always in debt. Another wants to be a poet and spends his days writing odes that no one wants to read. The only exception would seem to be Sir Brutus Jenkins's younger brother, who has a weakness for the gentler sex that costs the poor fellow an arm and a leg.

Nevertheless, I shall not give up on him. Tomorrow is another day, and another opportunity to persuade him from his folly. I always find that the attempt is apt to be somewhat exhausting. After bandying words with Sherlock, I did not feel up to the battle of wresting the fireside armchair away from Sir Hector Mamble. Eight-five years old the man may be, but he is not averse to throwing a sturdy right hook.

I do wish, however, he would refrain from picking his teeth with his fork at the dining table. It really does lower the tone.

Friday, 2nd January, 1880

They say a break is as good as a change, but the mood at Whitehall seemed not to have benefitted from our enforced break. The Prime Minister, Lord Kettleby, was fractious, the Home Secretary bumptious, the Foreign Secretary was nursing a sore head and the Chancellor of the Exchequer was his usual breezy self, that is to say full of hot air and bad breath.

Being a Friday, I was obliged in my official capacity as unofficial adviser – or *éminence grise* as Sherlock prefers to describe me – to attend the usual weekly meeting at Downing Street, and, this being the day after New Year, we achieved less than usual. The Home Secretary's Personal Private Secretary, Maurice Comely-Legge, a lean man with an acerbic face and an air of intelligence that sits ill with his professed general ignorance, for once redeemed himself by adding something of value to the conversation. It seems he was in Paignton visiting relatives over the festive period and caught the opening night of Mr Gilbert and Mr Sullivan's new offering, *The Pirates of Penzance*[1]. After telling us how much he enjoyed it, he then regaled us with a song from the piece.

I do not know how it sits with other men, but I am always somewhat embarrassed when a fellow bursts into song quite out of the blue. I hold too that a man who is privy to official correspondence on a daily basis should not be encouraged in such an enterprise, particularly when he has a teapot in one hand and a plate of Bath Olivers in the other. Nor does Comely-Legge have what one might call 'a fair voice'. When all these disparate factors mingled together, the result was not a happy one.

At the crescendo, Comely-Legge rose up on his toes and a liberal dollop of hot tea slopped out of the spout and scalded the cat. This poor creature, a sensitive soul who was already sulking due to the unwarranted assault on his finer sensibilities, took out his annoyance on the Foreign Secretary's shin. As sharp teeth sunk into his ankle, the poor fellow merely smiled sadly and shrugged. Such fortitude in the face of feline torment can only be the result of many years of patient suffering – he is, after all, a married man.

Even after all this, the debacle was still not at an end. For the grand finale, Comely-Legge gestured grandiloquently and succeeded in flinging all of the biscuits onto the Home Secretary's lap. That would not have been so bad had he not scooped up every last crumb from the man's trousers and then offered the plate to me.

---

[1] The first UK performance of *The Pirates of Penzance* took place at Paignton, Devon, on 30th December 1879.

One does not like to make a fuss about these things, but one must draw the line somewhere. And warm, bruised biscuits are most definitely my limit.

Having despatched Comely-Legge on an errand of no particular importance, for there is only so much a man's ears can take of strangled notes and muddled verses, the conversation fell to matters not of home and abroad as might be expected, but to Christmas and the New Year festivities.

There was not one man around that table who did not have a tale of woe to relate. The Foreign Secretary, Sir Ernest Gigglesthorpe, explained how he had come by his injury by taking liberties with this mother-in-law. It turned out that he had got rather merry on the port on New Year's Eve, and had given the lady a kiss on the cheek 'for the sake of Auld Lang Syne'. At this, she called him a drunken sot, thumped him with her umbrella, and told him not to make a nuisance of himself in the future. I daresay it is a lesson he will not soon forget.

It paints an unhappy picture of domesticity in Sir Ernest's house when one hears that his mother-in-law comes armed with her umbrella and is not slow to use it. Having met the lady – she has an acid tongue, which has been said to strip wallpaper at a hundred yards – I can only assume that he must have been very merry indeed to have attempted such a manoeuvre in the first place.

I am not one for these social pleasantries, although I am aware that it is expected. If I had my way, I should do what is required of me and go home. Social intercourse is demanded, however, as is an account of one's festive activities, for the purpose, one assumes, so that all might share in mutual commiserations and thus retire in the happy knowledge that no one had a better time than anyone else.

This knowledge makes me wary. I was expected to relate some seasonal horror. All I could think of was the occasion on

11

Christmas Eve when someone at the club spread the rumour that there was not enough coal to last us till Boxing Day. I am glad to say that it was wholly untrue, although it did cause consternation for a good ten minutes until the club secretary was able to give an account of the situation.

All I am willing to say of that unhappy drama is that whoever was responsible need not think that I have forgotten. When the identity of the offending member is discovered, he shall be asked to leave the Diogenes and never return.

"Do you mean to say," demanded Witherington-Smitherington, "that you did nothing over Christmas?"

Witherington-Smitherington – Withers for short – does something or other at the Treasury. From what I have been able to discover, he arrives in the morning, has his tea, walks his dog, has his lunch, reads the paper, has tea again and then goes home. I asked him once what it was exactly that he did. He said he was an assistant to the assistant of the assistant to the assistant's assistant who was Head Assistant of the Assistant to the Treasury Office. After the third 'assistant', my eyes had glazed over. I have not made the attempt again.

Having an undefined government position gives him the right to turn up at these weekly meetings, although one would wish he did not. Withers is one of those fellows who never tires of his own opinion. If the Chancellor is breezy, then he is windy, constantly giving all and sundry the benefit of his wisdom. I wish someone would tell him that such largesse is misplaced; given the collective intelligence gathered in this room, his advice is superfluous at best.

Now, and most annoyingly of all, he had hit upon that one subject which I had hoped to avoid. As I say, the man is a positive menace.

"Not nothing," I corrected him. "In fact, I passed Christmas and New Year at my club."

12

"Confound you, sir!" he retorted, the veins in his nose bulging in indignation. "That you alone should be allowed to enjoy yourself while the rest of us have had to endure the discomforts of the season is outrageous! If I am to suffer, then all should suffer. Let it be the common lot. This shirking of responsibility should be against the law. I shall write to my MP about it forthwith!"

Lord Kettleby reminded Withers that he *was* the Member of Parliament for his constituency and therefore he would have to write to himself. To this Withers stated that he never read anything his constituents sent him and that his secretary dealt with their 'whines and whinges'. In return, the Prime Minister remarked that it was no wonder that the voters held the government in such low regard if this was the attitude of their elected representatives.

If I thought this was an end of the matter, I was mistaken.

"Have you no family, Holmes?" Withers persisted. "Or did you desert them to wallow in self-indulgent solitude at this club of yours?"

As a general rule, I hold that a man's family is not a suitable subject for conversation over tea and biscuits. Especially, one feels, when the family in question is mine. I do not mind admitting that I have a younger brother, but beyond that, whenever possible, I disavow any kinship with any of the varied and scattered members of the Holmes clan. That they are out there, I know only too well, for they write when they can be bothered to remember my existence, which is usually when they want something, and then they threaten to visit.

I usually find the promise of sending money keeps them at bay or failing that the mention of an infectious illness. Great-Uncle Theodore successfully malingered for years and never saw a single member of his family from the age of forty till the day he died thirty-two years late. Indeed, his wife maintained that it was the shock of encountering his eldest son and future daughter-in-law in the drawing room one night after he had crept down to raid the kitchen stores that brought on his fatal seizure. One never knows about these things and I daresay there is an element of truth in it, especially knowing what his eldest son was like.

For the present, however, Withers had awakened the curiosity of the gathering. I was met with expectant glances all around.

"I knew an Aubrey Holmes at Oxford," said the Chancellor, Sir Herbert Bendish, chewing thoughtfully on his biscuit. "Queer fellow. When they asked him what he wanted to be in later life, he said eccentric."

"Is that a profession?" asked the Home Secretary, Lord Snoring.

"I would rather say it was a calling," said the Prime Minister.

"Any relation of yours, Holmes?" the Chancellor wondered.

"No, never heard of the fellow," I lied. The least said about Cousin Aubrey, the better in my opinion. "My only close relation is a brother."

"A brother?" queried Withers. "Older?"

"Younger, by seven years."

"You have mentioned something of him before, as I recall," said the Prime Minister. "His name is Sheerwater or Sheerness, something like that, isn't it?"

"Sherlock," I corrected him.

"I deplore this fashion for giving young men pretentious names," declared Withers, looking at me down the length of his nose. "It gives them airs above their station. It can only lead to loose living and immorality."

Coming from a man a name whose Christian name was Tantamount, I found the accusation somewhat hard to swallow.

14

"And what does this younger brother of yours do?" Withers demanded.

For once, I was lost for words. It is an unhappy experience, especially when it happens in the presence of men who direct the laws and governance of the land. In the event, the best I could do under the circumstances was to tell them the truth.

"I am glad you asked," I admitted, "for the worry of it troubles me day and night. The truth of the matter is that my younger brother has given himself over entirely to a life of crime."

"Disgraceful!" exclaimed Withers.

"My dear fellow, how inconvenient for you," said the Prime Minister in that paternal tone of his. "Yes, I do see now why you've been reticent about the subject. Mind you, I hear there's a lot of it about. What with the price of coal these days–"

"No," I interrupted before we had any misunderstandings. "He hasn't taken *up* crime, he wants to foil it in all its various guises."

"You mean he wants to solve mysteries?" said Lord Snoring, sucking hard at his pipe only to discover that the flame had gone out. "Has he ever said why?"

"Because it interests him," I replied.

"I've a mystery he can solve," spoke up Sir Ernest. "If he can tell me why my wife insists on adding tea to milk instead of milk to tea, which as everyone knows is the right way to go about it, I'll make it worth his while."

"I'll tell you for nothing," said the Chancellor sagely. "Is your china of good quality?"

"First rate."

"Then she has no concerns about the heat damaging her cups. Her persistence in this regard suggests that she does it because it annoys you."

"Why on earth would she want to do that?"

"Because the sole purpose of marriage, my dear fellow," said the Chancellor, "despite what you may have heard, is in having shackled yourself to one person for the rest of your life, you then proceed to test the limits of their endurance until one or the other parties grows bored of the exercise or dies, whichever comes first. The sooner you come to realise this, the easier your life will be. If I were you, I'd reciprocate. I find picking my teeth and drumming my fingers on the table irritates my dear wife terribly. I'd start with that, if I were you."

"What you need, Holmes," said Withers, raising his voice imperiously over this discussion of modern manners, "is to give that insolent young brother of yours a good hiding. I wouldn't tolerate behaviour like that from a brother of mine."

The thought had occurred to me. I had had occasion once to box Sherlock's ears when he was younger after he dropped a snake onto my head whilst I was conversing with a young lady. My reputation never quite recovered after that. A gentleman loses something in the eyes of the female fraternity when they discover he is able to scream louder than they do. Taking a similar line now was out of the question for he was old enough and big enough to retaliate.

"The army then," said Withers. "They'll knock some sense into him. They don't tolerate idle young men talking eyewash about solving mysteries in the military."

I struggle to see Sherlock in uniform. He has a disregard for authority which is lamentable. From whence it comes I do not know. Our dear father was the most upright man who ever drew breath, and would have continued to be so in the afterlife had our dear mother not insisted that he be buried lying on his back just like everyone else.

No, I hesitate to suggest the army to Sherlock. I am certain he would spend his entire career on a charge of insubordination and never once leave the barracks, which would keep him out of harm's way, certainly.

Besides, the men of the Holmes family have never thrived in the military. It is said that during the Civil War Great-Great-Great-Grandfather Ambrosius lost an arm to Cromwell, a leg to the King and his virtue to a woman in a London bawdy house. The loss of which of those troubled him the most, family legend does not recall.

However, I could see that this failure on my part to curb my brother's excesses was not going down well with the others. I sought to redeem myself in the only manner left to me, by bringing up Sherlock's intention to have 'a trade'. I could not have gained more sympathy had I been a homeless puppy.

"Most trying for you," consoled the Prime Minister. "But you must not lose heart, Holmes. One day your brother may see the error of his ways and realise the grief he has caused to you and so by degrees return to the bosom of his family."

"One can but hope, sir," I replied.

"Forbearance, Holmes. They do say that suffering is good for the soul, although personally I prefer cricket. Do you play?"

Then the conversation turned to all matters sporting and they lost their interest in me and my trials. The meeting ended, two hours later than usual, and I was able to return to the relative harmony of my club. I felt decidedly liverish that evening and before long, and to my dismay, I discovered I was suffering from those heralds of impending illness, namely a sore throat and aching head. In such circumstances, there is only one course of action. I took to my bed and resolved to stay there until things finally returned to normal on Monday.

Saturday, 3rd January, 1880

I awoke this morning with the certainty that my last hour had come. My head pounded, my throat was raw and I lacked the energy to rise from my bed, let alone hobble across the road to my club.

Sympathy from any quarter seemed to be in short supply. When I informed my landlady, the redoubtable Mrs Creswell – an Amazon of a woman, near six foot tall and somewhat broad in the beam – that very soon she would have to find a new tenant for these rooms of mine, she merely laughed.

"Oh, go on with you," said she. "You men are all the same, making a lot of fuss about a silly little cold. My late husband was just like you, Mr Holmes, always saying he was at Death's door because he had a headache or a belly ache or cramp in his leg. Then one day we were sat at breakfast and he says to me: 'Harriet, I've not felt this well in ages'. Not five minutes later dropped down stone dead. Now, Mr Holmes, what does that tell you?"

I was not sure what to make of this unedifying little story, unless it was meant as a warning against Mrs Creswell's breakfasts. I did say, however, that whatever her opinion of my condition, no one was a better judge than the afflicted when it comes to matters of health. I could only speak from my personal experience and was thus compelled to state with some certainty that my demise was imminent.

Mrs Creswell found this very amusing. To her credit, she did promise to return with soup and toast after she had finished attending to her cat, Madame Fluffy, who had been indisposed after eating a dozen pilchards the night before. Given what had happened to Mr Creswell and hearing of Madame Fluffy's troubles, I wondered whether I would be better advised to don my clothes and slip away to the safety of my club, where I have every confidence in the culinary skills of the chef. But since even sitting up in bed drained me beyond reason, escaping from Mrs Creswell's attentions was out of the question.

What I needed was a supporter at my side in this my darkest hour. My thoughts naturally turned to fraternal consolation.

Somehow – I shall not elaborate on the cost to my health in so undertaking the endeavour – I managed to make it to the window and haul it up. In the street below was an urchin bothering passers-by with the offer of shining their shoes. I thought to tempt him from his profitless enterprise with the promise of a shilling if he would leave his post and take a message from a dying man to his brother.

Evidently the price of hiring a messenger has gone up since I was a lad, for there was a good deal of haggling involved in what should have been a simple transaction. The impudent child said if the message was that important, then it should be worth more than a shilling; indeed, he suggested the sum of one guinea. Appalled, I returned that he should have been ashamed for accepting any token for undertaking an act of mercy, and that I had only thought to compensate him for his loss of work out of the goodness of my heart. This little fellow was having none of it, however, and stuck to his guns, declaring that he would be a disgrace to the good name of his ancestors if he settled for anything less than a sovereign.

Finally we struck our bargain at half a crown, which is an extortionate amount for simply running an errand, and I crawled back to my bed whilst he hurried away with a note I had composed for Sherlock. In retrospect, perhaps it was a little melodramatic. Perhaps I was not about to breathe my last, but that was the impression that had come to bear upon me. This was no ordinary, common or garden malady – it was typhus at the very least, of that I was convinced, and with complications.

I was also aware, from bitter experience, that Sherlock does not usually answer my summonses unless the situation is dire. Since I had a few things to say to him before I departed this life, I judged it best to get him to my side as quick as humanly possible. Whether he would consider my impending death reason enough to set aside whatever it was he was doing remained to be seen.

As it happened, I lay on my bed of pain and misery for some hours before my brother deigned to put in an appearance. Night was upon the city and the lamps had been lit when finally I heard a familiar step outside my door. Mrs Creswell, the bringer of salty soup and dry toast, showed him in and I summoned up what little energy I could muster to warn him not to draw near, lest he become infected with my contagion.

If I expected protestations to this, I was disappointed. "What's the matter with you now?" was all he could spare by way of sympathy.

It has not escaped me that my younger sibling displays a disregard for what might be described as a proper affinity with the finer feelings of his fellow man. One would not wish to be constantly overcome by an excess of emotion, but one feels that the ability to be roused, at the appropriate time and place, is a desirable quality. Women, I am told, find it most attractive, much in the same way, one supposes, as they are moved by the prospect of a new bonnet.

In the case of my brother, however, one cannot help but feel that he is lacking in that respect – in terms of rousing, I mean, not in his appreciation for new bonnets.

For this reason, I endeavoured not to be offended by his off-hand attitude to my condition. Others may find such a remark directed towards a dying man somewhat callous. But had Sherlock been anything other than his usual self, I should have been worried more for him and less for myself.

"What kept you?" I managed to croak.

"I was busy, Mycroft."

"Busy!" I cried, unable to contain myself. This was the revelation for which I had been waiting for many a year. "Oh, to hear such a word from your lips. I die a happy man knowing that you have found your place in the world. What were you doing, Sherlock?"

"If you must know, I was dismantling an aluminium crutch," said he, removing his hat and coat, and settling himself in my armchair to warm his hands before the fire. "A singular little mystery, Mycroft. It really was most fascinating. Perhaps you would care to hear the particulars?"

This was not what I had been expecting. "Do you mean to tell me," I said, with as much indignation as an expiring man may muster, "that while I lay here dying, you were working on one of your infernal *cases*?"

Sherlock, as ever, was dismissive of such a consideration.

"You are not dying."

"I am gravely ill, brother, I assure you. I have been struck down by some lamentable ague and am not long for this world."

"You exaggerate. You always do. Look what happened last year. You told everyone you had gout when in fact you had an ingrown toenail."

"This is worse, much worse," I groaned, sinking back onto my bed of pain. "Not that you would know what I have suffered these past few hours, being too involved with your aluminium crutch to care! I could have died waiting for you."

"Mycroft, does the term malingerer mean anything to you?"

"I am not malingering, Sherlock. I am dying!"

"Very well," he conceded. "You *are* dying. In that case, you won't object to my having father's watch."

He actually had the gall to reach for it. I snatched it from the bedside table away from his grasp.

"For shame, brother," I chided him. "At least have the decency to let my corpse cool before you rifle my possessions."

"Whether I have it now or later cannot possibly matter to you. Why do you need a watch? You cannot take it with you."

"That is irrelevant. Why this unseemly haste, Sherlock? You have father's second best watch."

"Do you know why he considered it his second best? Because it does not work."

"Nonsense. That is an expensive time-piece."

"I daresay it was, once. Now it is broken, over-wound I should say, and I do not have the money to have it repaired."

"Well, you cannot have mine."

"How very inconsiderate of you, Mycroft, as always. I need a reliable watch. Occasionally, I do need to reach my appointments on time."

"What 'appointments' do you have that require your

22

punctual attendance? On second thoughts," I said, "I would rather you did not tell me. What a man does not know cannot hurt him. I have a hard enough time of it now holding my head up in public. People think you are odd, Sherlock, I suppose you know that?"

"Coming from the people with whom you rub shoulders, Mycroft, to be considered 'odd' is something of a compliment. Compared to the rest of our family, I am relatively normal."

"Well, that is true enough," I conceded. "At least you aren't like Cousin Aubrey."

"Strange you should mention Aubrey," said he ominously. "I had Christmas greetings from him. He is threatening to come and visit."

"Good heavens!" I said, sitting up. "When?"

Sherlock smiled in that annoyingly smug manner of his. "You appear to have made a sudden recovery. Would you care to revise your prognosis of your condition?"

"If Cousin Aubrey does come visiting, that *will* be the death of me."

He was good enough to reassure me that Aubrey would not put in an appearance until late spring, apparently on account of his belief that one should not 'cast a clout' until May was out. Personally, I have never cast a 'clout', either in May or at any other time, but knowing Cousin Aubrey, he probably had sound reasons for doing so, which he would explain at great length and in great detail should I be unwise enough to ask.

By ten o'clock, I was feeling much improved – an altercation with Sherlock usually has that effect on me – and with the first splashes of sleet criss-crossing the glass of my window, I felt it incumbent upon me to send my brother on his way before conditions became too bad.

To this, Sherlock replied that he thought he should stay the night. I was moved by this gesture and what I took to be a genuine concern for my welfare. I was about to thank him for his

23

consideration and for this show of brotherly affection when he spoilt the moment by declaring that my rooms were much warmer than his and that he should be quite comfortable in the armchair… *if I didn't mind.*

In matter of fact, I did mind. I wanted to be ill in peace and having Sherlock cluttering up the place is not something I feel inclined to tolerate even when well. However, I flatter myself that as the elder, it is my duty to set my younger sibling a good example.

I did not, therefore, turn him out into the snow and leave him to shiver in that garret in Montague Street he calls home. Stay he did, under sufferance, and I made no attempt to encourage him to repeat the exercise by offering him either blanket or pillow.

One has limits, after all, especially where younger brothers are concerned.

Sunday, 4ᵗʰ January, 1880

I awoke feeling much better, to find that not only had Sherlock gone, but so had my breakfast and my clean collar. Had I not kept my watch clutched in my hand all night, I am sure he would have taken that too, annoying wretch that he is.

This is why I do not encourage visitors – not only do they take advantage of one's hospitality, but they over-excite my landlady, and in no good sense of the word.

Mrs Creswell was all atwitch when I sought her out to enquire whether another breakfast could be found for a recovering invalid. From what I could gather, her unfortunate state had been brought about by my brother. Several times she alluded to his being 'a nice young man' and twice told me what 'nice manners he had'.

This sort of talk worries me, for Mrs Creswell is what I would normally call a woman of good sense and, as a rule, 'nice' is not a word generally associated with my brother. Arrogant, certainly. Brusque, definitely. Nice, never, unless bandied about by women of a certain age who have met him but briefly. For my brother, when he makes the effort, I have observed has this effect on susceptible females. I would not say he was charming, but clearly he has something. Should he ever employ it to some use, he could make a fortune.

Why then, I had to ask myself, had Sherlock charmed my landlady into believing he was 'nice'? Why this extravagant effort? An alarming thought came to mind. Despite my refusal to provide him with bedding the night before, he had found the experience congenial enough to consider making it a permanent arrangement. If so, he had wasted his time.

Since it often falls to me to foot the bills for his way of life – the cost of idling seems to get more expensive every year – I feel I have a right to have a say in the matter. He does not like my interference, but he who pays the piper calls the tunes.

Call me churlish, but I am not partial to the idea of having to live under the same roof as Sherlock. I am rather fond of my lodgings, convenient as they are for my work and my club. If he moves in, no matter how 'nice' he at first appears, the veils would soon fall from Mrs Creswell's eyes and both of us would find ourselves homeless.

I therefore robbed her of her illusions by telling her that not only was he penniless, but that he was a scholar with loud and noisy friends and intolerable habits. I did not go into detail. Such things are best left to the imagination.

This seemed to disappoint her considerably. She thanked me for my consideration and then admitted, as I had suspected, that she had been considering letting him have the empty room above mine. The very thought sent a chill to my heart. Sherlock, tramping about above me all night! I believe I have had a lucky escape.

To avoid a repeat of the night before, I made the supreme effort of struggling over to my club. If Sherlock called – there was a slim chance he might, although I doubted he was that thoughtful – then he would find me absent from home and thus conclude that I was quite recovered. I further resolved that should I ever find myself dying in the future, I would wait until I was quite sure that life was near extinct before sending word to my sibling. That way I would save a fortune in breakfasts and collars.

If I had hoped for a quiet day, however, I was corrected in that erroneous assumption as soon as I set foot outside the door. The boy from yesterday had returned to his post under my window and had the gall to accost me as I emerged from the building.

Was I still dying, he wanted to know, only business was not too brisk that day and he had time to run me some more messages.

"Not at the rates you charge," said I.

I will not defile these pages by committing to paper the name he called me in return. I shall only say that it cast serious aspersions on my generosity and my father's morals.

I cannot remember the last time my temper was roused, for it is wearisome thing that leaves me quite exhausted for hours afterwards. On this occasion, however, I felt some display of indignation was appropriate. I have to control myself for I am informed by certain members of my family that I am in temperament rather too much like Uncle Barnstaple, who once became so heated that his moustache fell off.

Quite how that happened was never explained, except that it was always cited as a dire warning as to the consequences of immoderate behaviour. It was therefore a good thing for both of us that a passing constable heard what the lad said and sent him on his way with a clip around the ear and a warning not to have so much cheek in the future.

I sought sanctuary at the Diogenes after that, and nursed my nerves with a brandy, sated my hunger with a good lunch of pheasant and treated my cold toes to an afternoon of toasting before the fire. I went to bed that night safe in the knowledge that the room above mine was still empty and that my brother was at a safe distance in his own lodgings over in Bloomsbury.

Whitehall beckons tomorrow with yet another round of meetings with the Prime Minister. I find that for once I quite relish the prospect. After the trauma of the last few days, a return to work shall be positively restful.

Monday, 5ᵗʰ January, 1880

A day of rest does wonders for the health, especially when one is not plagued by unsympathetic younger brothers talking twaddle about aluminium crutches and trying to seduce my landlady into giving him board and lodging. It was thus with a brisk step – perhaps I exaggerate there – a *moderately* brisk step that I alighted from my cab and braved the several yards of chill January weather twixt the kerb and the door to my Whitehall office without incident.

Within, all was nearly back to normal after the interlude of the festive season. Greenery was still draped about the place – it being the custom to leave decorations undisturbed until Twelfth Night for fear of dire, if unspecified, consequences – and the wag who had hung a sprig of mistletoe over the Assistant Under-Secretary's door had yet to remove it.

I say 'wag' advisedly for it might have been the Assistant Under-Secretary himself. Sir Horace Wrangle is a man so uneasy on the eye that his friends are said to remove prize mirrors from their houses when he comes visiting for fear of what his reflection might do. Now I think about it, I do recall seeing him lingering about underneath the mistletoe for no apparent reason whilst wearing a most salacious expression on his face. Office gossip has it – not that I listen to such nonsense, but one cannot help but overhear – that our cleaning lady, Mrs Trubbshaw, wandered blindly into the man's trap a week before Christmas with unfortunate results, especially for Sir Horace, who spent several days thereafter skulking in his office nursing a black eye. Mrs Trubbshaw, I am glad to report, emerged unscathed from the incident.

At least that is what I had been led to believe. On entering my office, I had cause to doubt. Granted, the good lady could do little about the multifarious swags of holly and ivy – put up in my absence one afternoon by one of the junior clerks in a sudden fit of festive spirit – but I did feel that she could have swept the floor free of leaf litter and squashed berries. There was a strange smell too, which I traced to the waste bin where one of the clerks had deposited a half-eaten mince pie and the green crusts of well-chewed sandwich.

I am not an unreasonable man. I wish to spoil no one's enjoyment of the season, but I feel that standards must be upheld even in the midst of festivities.

I contend, for example, that food should not be left to rot and create ungodly miasmas, noxious to the happy digestion of one's breakfast. Nor should this fashion for bringing the garden into one's home and place of work blind one to the necessity for cleanliness. Nature is a most untidy creature and people would do well to remember that. Leave the tree to the forest and the holly in the hedge – that way, the unwary among us, myself included, would not have to spend Christmas being prickled in places too delicate to mention.

With Christmas over, there was no excuse for laxity. I have much respect for Mrs Trubbshaw – anyone who can keep the Assistant Under-Secretary under control certainly demands respect – but I was determined to remind her of her duties. Accordingly, I sent for her and some ten minutes later a woman appeared, mop and bucket trailing behind her.

"You're not Mrs Trubbshaw," said I.

"No, I'm Mrs Bright, sir," said this sad-eyed apparition. "Mrs Trubbshaw was my aunt. I'm doing the cleaning now."

"Was?" I queried. "Has something happened to her?"

Mrs Bright pulled a handkerchief from her sleeve and dabbed her eyes. "She's no longer with us, sir," she sniffed. "It was so sudden too."

This was grave news. I hoped it was nothing that the Assistant Under-Secretary had done to cause her sudden demise.

"My condolences for your loss," I said gravely. "Console yourself with the thought that she has undoubtedly gone to a better place."

"I'll take your word for it, sir. I've never been that fond of Worthing myself."

"Worthing?"

"Aye, sir, that's where she's gone – off to Worthing with her young man," explained Mrs Bright. "No good'll come of it, I'm sure. Have you ever been to Worthing, sir?"

I am glad to say that thus far I have been spared that particular experience.

"Do you mean to tell me she isn't dead?" I asked.

"Dead, sir? No, not her. Though she might as well be, given how she's upped sticks and gone after her fancy man, and him a seller of cockles and winkles on the seafront. The neighbours talk of nothing else. Taking off with a man of five-

31

and-twenty at her age, it isn't right. Now, sir, what was it you wanted?"

After such a revelation, I fear the wind was rather taken out of my sails, as the expression has it. Mrs Trubbshaw had been more than five-and-sixty. I can only assume that the encounter with the Assistant Under-Secretary had turned her mind. I shall have to remind him to keep his hands off the staff in future.

After that, I settled for a cup of tea from the distraught Mrs Bright, and spent the rest of the day reassuring the Prime Minister, who seemed to think something was afoot against him in the Commons. My other concern was for the morrow, and the day of my brother's birth[2]. As it happened, the problem of a gift was an elementary one. I have long learned to be suspicious of Sherlock's motives, but it seemed to me that our recent discussion about the state of his timepiece suggested a possible answer to the question.

From Whitehall, I went to my club, by way of Chiming and Bong, watchmakers to the trade. Above their door was a gleaming new Royal Warrant, and Mr Chiming was keen to regale me with an account of how he had supplied a time-piece that Christmas 'to a member of Her Majesty's household'.

He took great pride in telling me that he was not at liberty to divulge the identity of that exulted personage; all he was permitted to say was that this person moved 'in the same circles as Her Majesty'.

When I asked whether he was referring to Her Majesty's butler, Mr Chiming seemed quite taken aback and not a little offended that I had not set my sights higher. From this reaction, I concluded that I had been correct, perhaps inadvisably so, for it never does to put a craftsman in ill humour, particularly not if you wish to purchase his wares at a reasonable price.

---

[2] The diary confirms the traditional date for Sherlock Holmes's birthday as being 6th January.

"A watch, you say," said he when I put my request to him. "Well, Mr Holmes, you've come to the right place."

"Undoubtedly," I replied. "The last time I looked, it said 'watchmaker' outside."

Mr Chiming bowed. "That honour lies with Mr Bong, sir. I am but the humble seller of his fine goods. Now, sir, does the young lady's taste run to gold or silver?"

"In fact, Mr Chiming, it is for my brother."

"I see. Younger or older?"

"Younger."

"I am sorry to hear that," said Mr Chiming, shaking his head. "There's nothing quite like a younger brother for keeping a gentleman poor. He's lost his own watch, I take it?"

"No, he has one but it doesn't work."

"Mr Bong does excellent repair work."

"I was thinking of getting him something new. It is a gift."

"Ah, I see." He said it in a manner that suggested he understood rather too well, adding a knowing wink for good measure. "Going away, is he?"

"No, it is his birthday."

Quite what Mr Chiming had in mind I cannot say, except that the prospect of a simple birthday present seemed to have struck him as being rather mundane.

"Well, Mr Holmes, your brother, is he ostentatious?"

"He cannot afford to be on his present income."

"Careful with his possessions?"

"I wouldn't have thought so."

Mr Chiming considered. "Then what you need is a watch with a full case. No half measures if he is inclined to be clumsy, otherwise the glass will be broken in no time at all."

It took some deliberation, but I believe I chose the sort of watch suitable to a man of Sherlock's years and upbringing: a

33

plain gold case, with a tasteful inscription for sixpence extra – to be completed by the elusive Mr Bong – and a gold Albert chain to match. It was, so Mr Chiming assured me, the watch of a gentleman.

I said by way of jest that it would give my brother something to which to aspire. Unfortunately it fell on stony ground and I fear, by the way Mr Chiming snatched the watch from my hand and clutched it to his bosom as though protecting a small child, that I had created the impression that we were a family of uncouth philistines. He did assure me, however, that it would be ready for collection the next day, and I left to the sound of his heartfelt sobbing.

Tuesday, 6ᵗʰ January, 1880

The greenery has gone from the office, which is a blessing, and Mrs Bright has proved to be most diligent in her cleaning routine. I found just the one dropped berry, and that had rolled under the carpet in the furthermost corner of the room. Considering the state of the place yesterday, I feel I should not be so churlish as to point out this one omission. She is doing her best, under trying circumstances, and one should make allowances. Should any of my maiden aunts decide to elope with seafood sellers to Worthing, I am not sure I could bear it quite so stoically.

Instead of harrying the dear lady over one lost berry, I thanked her for her time and attention. At this, she smiled coyly and said it was nice to be appreciated. I considered that an end of the matter, but perhaps my intentions had been misread, for an extra biscuit appeared with my afternoon tea. I shall have to be more careful in the future, for I appear to have made a favourable impression on the lady. An extra biscuit today, but what of tomorrow?

As to business, there has been much talk of the upcoming general election. The mood of the country can never be gauged with any great accuracy – the voters are too capricious for that – but I had a message from Lord Kettleby asking for my opinion as to how matters stood. Personally, I foresee troubled times ahead and told him so. To this end, he asked if I knew of any jobs for decayed former Prime Ministers.

It is not the frame of mind in which I should set out to fight for my political survival, but, as Sherlock is fond of telling me, I have little in the way of ambition, and so am hardly in a position to criticise others.

Be that as it may, I feel some optimism would not go amiss, even if it is misplaced.

The pressing business of the day was of course Sherlock's birthday. On this day twenty-six years ago, my life was turned upside down by the arrival of a brother. Instead of a promised puppy, what I got was a bawling, red-faced, writhing mass of arms and legs that has grown up to be the bane of my life and has kept me poor ever since our dear father decided that it was time to shrug off his mortal coil.

I say decided, for he was a most awful ditherer and could never make up his mind about anything. The one time he was certain about anything proved to be his last. "This beef will be the death of me," he declared over supper one night, and he was right. Ten minutes later, his heart gave out and he succumbed, a bill from the butcher for £3.12s.6d. in one hand and a jar of pickled onions in the other.

A bill of that sum is enough to send anyone into an apoplexy, but what he intended to do with the onions is anyone's guess.

Sherlock and I have debated the matter many a time, and

neither of us has ever arrived at a satisfactory answer. The best theory I can postulate is that he intended a show of strength by opening the jar unaided – but why a jar of pickled onions when there were other items at hand is not so easily explained.

Well, we shall never know for certain. Perhaps that is for the best. A man should retain an air of mystery, after all.

On the subject of mysteries, the greatest of them all – what my brother did to fill his time between sleeping and eating – came somewhat closer to being solved when I saw an article in *The Times* about a thief who had devised an ingenious method of hiding his ill-gotten gains by secreting them within an aluminium crutch.

Since Sherlock had been babbling about crutches whilst I had been on my deathbed, I had to assume that this was the business that had detained him so long after I had sent word of my imminent demise. To my consternation, however, there was no mention of my brother in connection with the solution of the case or the apprehension of the thief, full credit going to a Scotland Yard detective named Lestrade.

This seems the height of bad manners to me. If one is to sacrifice one's brother for the sake of the criminal justice system, at the very least one might expect to find one's name in the press. To accept less is to trivialise human existence.

I meant to put this to Sherlock when he finally deigned to honour me with his presence at the club. When he wandered in half an hour late, he seemed out of sorts and unresponsive. I left him to his own devices, taking the view that the realisation that one is yet another year older and another year closer to death is hardly something warranting a celebration.

As a dutiful brother, I saw that he was fed and watered and then tried to lift his mood by playing our usual game of observation and deduction.

"Now what do you make of these fellows, Sherlock?" said

I, gesturing to a group of musicians who had taken up position in the street opposite to the window. For the best part of half an hour, they had been regaling pedestrians with a tuneless version of *The Miller of Dee*, complete with a dullard youth who had forgotten the words and a howling dog who valiantly tried to accompany him.

"A curious group, wouldn't you agree?"

Sherlock gave them a fleeting, listless glance. "Cordwainers," he muttered.

"You deduced that from the careful stitch-work of their boots and the calluses on their hands caused by the handle of the leatherwork's hammer, no doubt."

"That and the board saying they are collecting for 'The Shoemakers' Benevolent Society'."

It has not escaped my notice that my brother has a lamentable inclination towards flippancy. It ill behoves a gentleman, and by extension a gentleman's son, to sully his wits in these lower forms of humour. Heaven knows I have tried, but in Sherlock's case, I fear my best efforts to steer him from this course have fallen on stony ground.

"I had hoped you would look beyond the obvious, my dear boy," said I. "The youth, for instance, is clearly the son of the man with the cornet, for the shape of the brow and turn of the mouth is quite distinctive, as is his habit of holding his head to one side, a sure sign of—"

"Mycroft, I daresay you are correct," said Sherlock, interrupting me quite unnecessarily. "But you will forgive me if I say I am not in the mood for a discussion about cordwainers and inherited eccentricities."

So saying, he sank back into silence, his chin resting on his chest and the black cloud of misery hanging about him. I am used to my brother's moods, but this seemed to be something of a different species.

I had good cause to be concerned. Our hall porter had only that afternoon brought to my attention an article in the newspaper about a mysterious malady affecting several young men of Sherlock's age, who had died with their feet in a state of disarray. For a man who spends his working day upright, I consider him to an authority on the subject. As he has often said, without good feet, a man 'doesn't have leg to stand on'.

Now I looked a little closer at my sibling, I noticed that his skin looked somewhat yellow, although that may have been due to the livid glow of the gaslight. He was pinched and thin – again, his normal state – and was blue-black about the eyes with tiredness, a rare feat for someone who spends so much time in bed. All this taken together suggested the worst of possibilities.

"Are you ill?" I asked him.

It was all he could do to muster a shake of his head.

"Is it your feet?"

He gave me an unfriendly glare. "My what?"

"Your feet, sir. Are they in a state of disarray?"

"Mycroft, I'm not discussing my feet with you."

"Then you do not deny that it is the source of your problems. Sherlock, this cannot be ignored. Why, your very life is in peril if the papers are to be believed. I have the name of an excellent doctor—"

"Whatever are you talking about?" said he insolently, his tone suggesting in the most insulting manner that I was somehow at fault. "You're not becoming woolly-minded, are you?"

"Certainly not. I am, however, concerned for your health."

"There is nothing wrong with my health. If you must know, I am bored."

"Bored? What the devil do you have to be bored about?"

Perhaps I was sharp with him. That did not excuse his scowling at me.

"I have nothing to occupy my mind at present," said he.

"My last case came to a successful conclusion and I have had precious little since."

"This would be the business with the aluminium crutch?"

He brightened fractionally. "You remembered."

"I read about it in the newspaper. Your name did not appear, I note."

"No reason why it should. I play the game for the game's sake."

"Not for glory?"

"Well, a little would not go amiss."

"Or profit?" To that he said nothing, which could mean only one thing. "You did get paid, I take it?"

He responded by variously staring out of the window, biting his nails and brushing lint from his trousers. I know my brother well enough to recognise the signs of procrastination when I see them.

"Sherlock, really. This will not do. You have not the resources to take on cases for charity. You need money, unless you intend to live on rainwater and fresh air for the rest of your life." It seemed the ideal moment to press my case, given that I had the upper hand. "Well now, you say you are bored. There is vacancy in my office for—"

"I am not *that* bored," said he, sniffing disparagingly. "If you are going to be tiresome about this, Mycroft, I shall leave."

"I have no wish to stifle you, but it grieves me to see you squander your talents in this profitless way."

"It is not profitless to me."

"Indeed. How do you propose to pay the rent this month?"

He sighed and acted as though such things were beneath him. I despair for him at times. What will happen to him should I die unexpectedly like Father, with or without the jar of pickled onions to hand, I dread to think.

"I suppose I shall have to pay it, *as usual*," I said.

"One day, I will pay you back. Until then, I understand that your landlady has an empty room—"

"It has been taken," I said quickly before he got any ideas in that direction. "Sherlock, let us not quarrel. We are orphans, you and I, the surviving remnants of a once great and glorious bloodline."

"Do not throw the ancestors at me again, Mycroft. I'm not in the mood. And we are hardly the last – you seem to forget Cousin Aubrey."

I reminded him that one could not possibly forget Cousin Aubrey, try as one might. "What I mean to say is that you are my brother, the only one I am likely to have now our parents are deceased. Furthermore, it is your birthday, and I have a small token for you."

I had sent one of the junior clerks to collect the watch from Chiming and Bong that morning. Given Mr Chiming's reaction the day before, I judged it wiser not to put in an appearance myself. When I saw Sherlock's reaction, however, I had to wonder why I had bothered to go to so much trouble.

"It's rather small," said he, taking it from the box and dangling it before his eyes.

Expressions of gratitude do not come easily to our family. It can be traced back to Great-Grandfather Hezekiah, five times removed, who once thanked a pretty maid and then had to marry her.

Still, I would have liked some indication that my gift was well received.

"You ungrateful little devil," I said. "Is that the best you can do?"

"No, it's very thoughtful of you, Mycroft. Much appreciated."

"Better. Have you seen the inscription?"

He opened the case and peered at the engraved words.

41

"*Tempus fudgit*'. Does that have any significance?"

"Don't be obtuse. It says *'Tempus fugit'* – 'time flies' in Latin. Any school boy could tell you what that means."

We batted the issue back and forth for an unseemly length of time before we resolved the matter by my inspecting Mr Bong's handiwork. As much as I hate to admit it, Sherlock was right. Mr Bong had inserted a surplus letter and had thus rendered my carefully considered inscription as so much nonsense.

"I shall take it back and have it corrected," I said. "This is intolerable."

"No, Mycroft, that will not be necessary. I am more than happy to have '*Tempus fudgit*'. It makes this watch unique. I feel confident that there is not another quite like it anywhere in London."

My brother may make light of it, but I am not so easily placated. I shall have a few words to say to Mr Chiming and Mr Bong when next I call in. Royal Warrant they may have, but a Latin dictionary would be of more use.

Tempus fudgit indeed.

Monday, 1st March, 1880

I resolved when I began this journal that I would record the events of my life, significant or otherwise. The problem with such an approach is how one is to decide what is significant and what is not. Since my last entry, I cannot say that anything particularly singular or noteworthy has happened, which accounts for the many empty pages between this entry and the last.

However, today, finally something of significance has occurred. Two words shall suffice: Victoria Sandwich.

As a general rule, I enjoy a piece of cake as much as the next man. There is something intrinsically pleasing about the combination of jam and cream sandwiched between two generous layers of sponge cake. It is the sort of fancy that one must take one's time to enjoy – it is an indulgence, one might say, and not to be squandered. There is a time and a place for everything, not least because discovering one has icing sugar on one's chin during a meeting with the Prime Minister is liable to cause much embarrassment for one's self and great amusement amongst the junior clerks.

It is entirely the fault of Mrs Bright. The usual biscuit with my eleven o'clock tea swiftly developed into two shortbreads until we ended last month with a plate piled high. The whispering this has caused in the office rose to such unhealthy levels that I have been obliged to ask Mrs Bright to desist. She managed to bide by my order for several days. Then this morning appeared the dreaded Victoria Sandwich.

It came with a knowing wink and Mrs Bright's most winning smile. She told me she had made it herself and hoped I would enjoy it. Furthermore she added that she liked a man with a good appetite, for it put her in mind of her dear old Edward, God rest him, who could eat like ten men, if not work like them.

I ate the cake, hating as I do to waste good food, but it is as I feared. The woman has developed an attachment to my good self through no fault of my own. Several times now she has mentioned that she is a widow and never had any complaints from her late husband about her housekeeping and cooking. I daresay this is true, but why she would think that I am in need of a wife, I cannot say. That I leave to the rest of the world and my brother, although if he ever shows any inclination in that direction and provides me with a niece or nephew I shall be greatly, and pleasantly, surprised.

It is evident to me that I must dissuade Mrs Bright from this erroneous course, which may prove easier than I feared, for events are moving most unfavourably in government. A general election is upon us and none of the present incumbents are hopeful of retaining their political offices. At my meeting with the Prime Minister earlier, he stated his certainty of defeat without attempting to deceive either me or himself. For that, one must admire him; there is little use in denying these things, and whatever is to happen must be faced.

"This may be the last chance we ever get to talk like this, Holmes," said he. "I want you to know that I have valued your sage advice over these past few years. You have a unique mind and your grasp of political affairs is unsurpassed."

"Thank you, Prime Minister," I replied. "I hope I shall continue to serve you in that capacity."

He shook his head. "Not with me you won't. By the end of April, I have every reason to believe that there will be another in this seat – and you know what his opinion is of me. You may be sure that if we lose this election, there will be a cull in these offices. Off with the old and on with the new. It goes without saying that anyone associated with the present administration will be replaced."

"Even Withers, sir?"

"*Especially* Withers, if he can't give a good account of what it is he actually does around here. Has he ever told you?"

"Not specifically, Prime Minister. I did ask him once but he fell to mumbling and I did not like to give the impression that I was hard of hearing."

"Ah, well, perhaps my successor will have better luck. As for you, Holmes, I shall give you a good reference, not that I suppose for one instance that it will do you any good. However, the Leader of the Opposition is not a man who would cut his nose to spite his face, as the saying has it. Doubtless he will recognise your particular abilities. But..." He paused meaningfully. "I cannot guarantee it. You do understand what I am saying?"

"That my employment at Whitehall could cease. Yes, sir, I understand."

"He would be a fool if he let you go, but there's no reasoning with the man. Would it be a hardship? You do have independent means."

"Limited," I admitted. "Not enough to keep one soul, let

45

alone two."

The Prime Minister frowned. "How is that brother of yours? Still trying his hand at solving mysteries?"

"Yes, and not very successfully. He has been tormented by ennui these past two months because he tells me he has nothing decent on which to concentrate his mind."

"I despair of young people today," he sympathised. "In my day, the young were not allowed to be bored. We had to make our own amusement or give good reason why not. I blame this modern age. These newfangled inventions encourage idleness. I did hear only the other day that we are importing frozen meat from Australia[3]."

"It can only benefit the poor, Prime Minister, by reducing prices."

"As you say, Holmes, but mark my words, it is the thin end of the wedge. Only the other day my Personal Private Secretary had the gall to ask me whether I wanted my name included in a directory for people with telephones[4]. I ask you, what is the world coming to? Very soon, the need to meet anyone face to face will be replaced by this notion of speaking to them from afar. What next – a telephone you can carry about with you? What an inconvenience that would be! It's bad enough having so many calls on one's time as it is without being at people's beck and call from dawn to dusk. No, if you ask me, this obsession with telephones will never catch on. It will go the way of moustache protectors and wooden legs for donkeys – a passing fad."

The upshot of this meeting, the question of telephones, moustache protectors and wooden legs aside, was that I have had

---

[3] The first frozen meat arrived in Britain from Australia aboard the SS *Strathleven* on 2nd February 1880.

[4] The first telephone directory was published by the London Telephone company on 15th January 1880. It contained 248 entries.

to face the uncomfortable truth that very soon I might find myself unemployed.

It is a worrying situation. I have had a position at Whitehall ever since coming down from Oxford. I had progressed from one to the other as does an infant from mother's milk to father's toffee creams. I know no other life. What else would suit me so tolerably?

I worried and vexed over the coming turbulence for the rest of the day so that by the time Sherlock found me at the club I was out of humour and not at all interested in his tales of arsenic in relation to the history of crime and its detection. I was perhaps a little harsh on him, but I had had further bad news that day and was feeling its effects.

"Has anyone ever told you, Sherlock, that this interest of yours in poisons is positively morbid?" I said querulously. "It seems to me that you dwell too much on death and not enough on life."

"Such knowledge is essential to my trade," said he unconcernedly.

"Must you call it 'a trade'? The man our father employed as a chub fuddler called himself a tradesman."

"My profession then."

"A profession of which you are the only representative."

"Every profession had to start with one member," he said, not unreasonably.

"Why are you in such a foul temper? Was it the beef? I thought it a trifle overdone."

"No, it was not the beef. If you must know, I have had a communication from a member of the family."

"Not Cousin Aubrey?" said he, starting from his chair.

Such is the man's reputation that he has eclipsed all other members of our sprawling family. On this occasion, however, he had been outdone by another.

I should clarify this by saying that, on our father's side, the members of the Holmes family are many and various. Our relatives are liberally distributed across the country, neither close enough to be an inconvenience nor distant enough to be forgotten. Only when they make their presence felt by writing to tell us of their good news do they become a nuisance.

"No, I have had a letter from Cousin Masterman. He has had a baby."

"Remarkable," said Sherlock, marrying it with that insolent look of his. "He must be the talk of the medical world."

"Tut, brother! His wife has had the baby of course. He has had—"

"The worry and expense?"

It has not escaped me that Sherlock has a tendency to sneer at those things for which other men pine and hanker. Tell him that someone has fallen in love, he says it is a temporary imbalance in the brain's normal functions. Tell him that someone is to marry, he expresses his condolences. Tell him that someone has had a baby and he positively recoils, as though one had suggested he thrust his hand into a pit of vipers or – heaven forbid! – find himself respectable employment.

This does not bode well. We are a family of two, myself being the heir as the eldest and Sherlock as the youngest being the spare. If between us we cannot conjure up at least one wife and one child, I fear we shall have failed in our duty to continue the line. Had our dear father adopted the same attitude, we should not be here today. Considering he was the most experienced practitioner of procrastination who ever lived, if he could manage it, then I daresay so must we.

One of us will have to turn our minds to it one day. For myself, finding the time is my greatest stumbling block. That, and the thought of having to make the effort of wooing a prospective bride. If the whole business could be done and dusted in a week, I

48

might find the energy to rouse myself. But engagements these days seem to go on for years. I do not have the endurance for a lengthy affair. How others manage it, I cannot say. By the time these couples do manage to wed, I am sure they must have forgotten what the attraction was in the first place.

"If you had let me finish," said I reprovingly, "I was going to say he has had a son."

"Good for him. Why does he think that would interest you?"

"Because he has asked me to be a godparent."

Sherlock stared at me and then began to laugh heartily. "Forgive me, Mycroft," said he, trying to catch his breath, "but you are an unlikely candidate as godparent. When did you last speak to Masterman? He has only asked you because he hopes you will give the child a decent christening gift. Tell him you are otherwise engaged and decline."

"How very cynical of you, brother," I said, offended that any thought of monetary consideration might be behind this request. Knowing Cousin Masterman, however, I did not entirely discount the notion. "You should know that I intend to accept this honour. One does not simply refuse a sacred duty. As for Masterman's reasons, why, I am perfectly respectable. Can you think of anyone more suited to the role?"

"And how, Mycroft, do you intend to fulfil your obligations as a godparent? You never leave that chair, save to waddle to Whitehall and back."

I am sorry to say that my brother has no grace about him. He will invariably say the first thing that comes into his head, regardless of consideration for his fellow man's finer feelings.

"*Waddle*? Are you suggesting that I am stout?"

"No, you are rotund, which is quite a different matter. Every time I see you, you appear to have added another inch to that girth of yours, which must please your tailor no end."

"What does that have to do with my being a godparent?"

"As I understand it, you have to promise to renounce sin. Do you honestly think you could renounce gluttony?"

"I am not a glutton," I said, now deeply affronted by his remarks. "I am an epicure."

"An epicure who eats too much."

"It is not my fault that my constitution tends towards the sluggish. In any case, there is nothing to say that a man of generous proportions cannot be a godparent. If so, that would discount over half the male population."

"Well, I hope you know what you are doing, Mycroft. These family gatherings are always fraught."

"You exaggerate, Sherlock. What can possibly go wrong at a christening?"

"You do remember what happened at Great-Aunt Mildred's funeral?"

I did. It was a disastrous affair. Cousin Cornelius had toppled into the open grave when no one was looking and later rose up as the mourners were gathering, much to everyone's distress and consternation. Cousins Daphne and Daisy had a fight amongst the tombstones because they were wearing the same hat, and Aunt Matilda called the vicar 'a dithering old fool' for taking too long with the ceremony.

There is a good reason why the varied members of our family do not mingle so. It is because we do not rub along easily at all. Our ancestral history is riddled with cautionary tales of the dangers of getting too many of us together in one room. Duels have been fought before now over the meanest of slights – and that was only the women.

Someone once commented that the Wars of the Roses were as nothing compared to the Wars of the Holmeses, and it was for that reason that I was taking no chances. I had been asked to perform this duty and I intended to do so, but not without taking precautions.

"I had hoped that at such a happy event, you might be persuaded to join me, seeing as how you have nothing better to do with your time at the moment."

Sherlock almost choked on his tea. "I do not lack pluck," said he, "but I would rather endure the chef's braised lamb at the Diogenes club than attend this christening."

"What the devil is wrong with the lamb?"

"What is *right* with it? That is, if it is lamb. I should say it is an imposter, Mycroft, a wolf in lamb's clothing."

"You have never mentioned this before, Sherlock. If you had, I should have taken it up with the committee. I should certainly have refused to pay the bill. However, as regards the matter at hand," I said, sad that it had to come to this, "if you will not come of your own volition, then by coercion."

For once, he looked genuinely alarmed. "You would not dare."

"Wouldn't I? Your rent is due at the end of the week. As much as I hate having to resort to such methods, I fear you have forced my hand."

He scowled at me. "You will play that card once too often."

"Friday it is then. St Mary's Church in Finchley at noon. Do make yourself presentable. And try to smile. If you embarrass me before our relations, I might never forgive you."

"If it means never having to associate with any of them ever again, it might be worth it."

I hoped he was jesting, but one can never tell with Sherlock. Friday will prove to be very interesting indeed.

Friday, 5th March, 1880

Posterity shall record that Friday was a glorious spring day, cloudless but not too bright, warm but not uncomfortable, fresh but not too cold. Overall, an excellent day for a christening.

A shame then that the ceremony took place inside a gloomy Georgian edifice, all sterile stone and pudgy-faced cherubs, with a clergyman so ancient that he creaked as he walked. Cousin Masterman, whittled down to painful thinness by years of constant worry about his younger brother – a fate that I hope I may be spared, heaven willing – was pleased that I had accepted the role of godparent and was somewhat over-enthusiastic in expressing his gratitude, even having the gall to shake my hand and tell me what a pleasure it was to see me.

I thought this forward for a man I had not seen in over twenty years, but after having met the other godparents, I saw his reasoning. His wife's family were *odd* to put it kindly, a rare achievement in itself when compared to the foibles of our family.

They shared the same small eyes and pinched cheeks, as though permanently chewing over their grievances and not liking the taste it left in their mouths. They spoke little, except to express their disdain, which was universal. The church did not please them, the vicar did not please them, and we, as a family, certainly did not please them.

From what Masterman told me, they had made their fortune from cutlery – his wife's grandfather had done something extraordinary with scrap metal – and they had sought respectability by marrying into 'old money' and our even older name. Unfortunately, they had not taken into account our associated baggage of precocious children and eccentric adults. The pained expression on all their faces throughout the afternoon spoke of their thwarted ambitions for the match. They were, although I hate to say it, the most appalling snobs.

I cannot speak for the rest of the family, but at least Sherlock and I did our best to uphold the family honour. We certainly looked the part, not that I doubted my brother would disappoint me in that respect because I had given him the money to attire himself suitably. Certain of our cousins disported themselves in rough country tweeds with countryside odours to match, which even for Finchley was considered beyond the pale. When water came to Aunt Emily's eyes, it was not because of the touching ceremony, but because Uncle Gordon had trailed something down the nave on the sole of his boot.

This is not to deny that the service was moving, and a family of softer sentiments or fewer pretensions might well have been moved to genuine tears. This is not our way, however; no sooner had the child's head been wetted then Cousin Clarence announced that it was 'high time that we all had something to drink'.

I did my duty by the child and solemnly promised to guide

young Wenceslaus Randle Enoch Nicholas Carey Holmes through the trials and tribulations of life to the best of my ability, a task which would prove difficult considering that a distance of near 200 miles would separate his new home from mine. But it was to overcome obstacles such as these – and I daresay for a few other reasons besides – that the Royal Mail was created. With the aid of that excellent institution, I am determined to be a conscientious, if absent godparent.

After that, with Cousin Clarence thirstier than ever, we took his suggestion and retired to Masterman's family home for the christening breakfast. It was a fine affair with the usual array of sandwiches, cakes and dainties, all laid out in the spacious 'Garden Room'. I daresay it was called that because it looked out upon the garden, which was pretty enough, if left in places to go the way Nature intended. What Masterman's in-laws would have called it was another matter – something less than complimentary if the disparaging look on his wife's mother's face was any indication.

We divided into ranks, his in-laws on one side of the room, sneering and whispering amongst themselves, and us on the other, opining, shouting, eating, chattering, sniping and generally rubbing each other up the wrong way. It could only end in disaster. We were as a powder keg, awaiting the spark. When it would come, we did not know, save that come it must. So many Holmeses in the same room was a guarantee of trouble.

To our credit, it started off calmly enough. The presence of the child kept the more unruly elements in check and gave the women something other to think about than themselves. Cousins Daphne and Daisy stopped their bickering about both having turned up wearing the same shoes and instead cooed over the baby, uttering the sort of nonsensical words that can only impair a child's intelligence.

Cousin Clarence, always a thoughtless soul at the best of

time, between dividing his time between fruit cake in one hand and cucumber sandwiches in the other, suddenly declared to everyone's consternation that it was an ugly baby and would grow into an ugly child and an even uglier adult. His sparring companion, Cousin Tollemarche, waded into the debate by saying that Clarence was the living proof of the truth of that assertion. This resulted in a heated discussion, from which I sought sanctuary with Cousin Masterman by the French windows where Sherlock looked in dire need of being rescued from the attentions of Cousin Esmeralda.

A curious young woman, all tombstone teeth, poor eyesight and wiry hair, Esmeralda – Esme for short, for she certainly lacks something where height is concerned – has always carried something of a torch for my brother. Quite why, neither he nor I can say. Sherlock assures me he has not encouraged her in this attachment, and I believe him.

I know certain of the family who would approve of such a match, for they are cousins most uncousinly in terms of close kinship, but it is not something I would encourage, even if Esme's feelings were reciprocated. The man who would marry Esme must be in want of a wife who, like ivy, clings and smothers in equal measure, and is infernally difficult to remove once taken root. Such a situation would not suit my brother at all.

On such occasions, one feels compelled to act – not least because it was my fault that he was there at all. Esme was not pleased by the interruption, but smiled sweetly enough – as sweetly as a girl with chapped lips may without splitting them further – and offered her congratulations to the happy parent.

"I am sure I would make an excellent mother," she added, casting a meaningful look in the direction of her affections.

"He's a bonny lad," I assured Masterman. "You must be proud."

"Very," said he, beaming in that manner reserved for the

exclusive use of new fathers. "I'm glad you came, Mycroft. It's good to see you."

"And I you, old fellow. Has life been treating you well?"

He paled and his skin took on that sickly, sallow hue of the troubled. "Well enough. Things were difficult for a while with the in-laws but they seem to have accepted me now."

"Accepted you? By George, they should have welcomed you with open arms."

Masterman shook his head sadly. "I love Martha, but not her family. Her mother dislikes me immensely."

"You did not marry the mother, Masterman dear," said Esme unhelpfully. "Rest assured, I would permit nothing to come between my husband and me."

"All the same, I would prefer to have her good opinion of me. She tolerates me to my face. What she says about me behind my back, heaven only knows. I had hoped that meeting the family might change her mind about me."

I glanced over to where Tollemarche was attempting with gusto to thrust a custard tart up Clarence's nose, much to the general delight and encouragement of our aged aunts and uncles.

"A terrible waste of food," I said. "If you don't mind me saying, Masterman, it was sheer folly on your part, thinking to impress your in-laws in this manner."

"Impress them? Oh, dear me, no. I wanted them to see that there are worse candidates for husbands than me." He smiled as Clarence turned the tables and pressed the tart firmly into Tollemarche's face. "I knew the family wouldn't let me down on that respect."

The contest came to an end and both sides retreated to lick their wounds free of egg custard and pastry crust.

"You'll understand, one day, when you marry, Cousins," said he. "Are either of you...?"

"Not at present," I said hurriedly, seeing a hungry gleam

come into Esme's eyes. "My current circumstances do not lend themselves to matrimony."

"And you, Sherlock?"

Since he had asked him outright, I could not very well reply. I only hoped he would be kind.

"I shall never marry," he declared, flaring his nostrils in that disdainful way of his when forced to address any of the normal concerns of his fellow man, "lest it bias my judgement."

Esme's face fell.

"Good heavens, quite a statement, Cousin." Masterman was perplexed by this, as well he might be. "But surely there is something to be gained from the meeting of two like minds and the joy such a union may produce."

"The disadvantages outweigh the benefits. Union with one person is limiting to the imagination and therefore destructive to the realisation of one's true potential. The selfish man may serve a higher purpose than the selfless one."

Esme's bottom lip began to tremble.

"The common lot of mankind has few attractions for me. What value is the happiness of one man when set against the misery and despair of all men? Don't you agree, Cousin Esmeralda?"

At times my brother can be quite heartless. Like a steam train emerging from a tunnel, the poor girl let out a wail that was painful to the ears and promptly left the room.

"I do wish she wouldn't make that noise," Masterman chided. "She'll wake the baby."

"She was always highly-strung, even as a child," I said, giving my brother a reproving look for his bluntness. "Something to do with art in the blood, I expect."

"If that is the result, I shall endeavour to cultivate common sense in my son," said Masterman, gently rocking the slumbering babe in his arms. "But tell me, Sherlock, do you mean to say that you wouldn't like one of these of your own one day?"

"I do not deny they have their uses," said he. "Several weeks ago, I had to disguise myself as an expectant mother—"

"How is that younger brother of yours?" I said to Masterman, moving the subject hastily on. "He isn't here, I notice."

"No, he's… away. Unavoidably detained at Her Majesty's pleasure." He almost blushed. "So, as you can see," said he, glancing about the room, "we are less than our usual complement. Cousin Aubrey couldn't make it either."

"Most unlike him. He could never turn down the offer of a free meal. What was his excuse?"

"He's chained to the railings at Waterloo Station into his second week of a protest against the railways. He wants them banned. He says people were a lot happier when it took them several days to reach their destination, because by the time they got there, it was time to go home again. Thus, no one ever outstayed their welcome and the thought of the journey discouraged travel, so people saw a lot less of their troublesome relations."

"Aubrey always was an original thinker," said Sherlock. "How long does he intend to keep up his campaign?"

"That rather depends on whether he can remember where he put the key to his padlock. The police have refused to help on the grounds that they feel safer knowing where he is." I was sure I saw the flicker of a smile come to his face. "Cousin Aubrey could be away from us for a very long time."

"Then in the most grievous of misfortunes, there may yet be some good," said I.

"Indeed." A fleeting expression of pain passed across his face and he folded at the waist. "Mycroft, would you care to hold your godson? There's something to which I must attend."

With that, he had passed me the slumbering child and

fairly darted out of the room. I had a suspicion it was something to do with the baked trout, the smell of which was near to pervading the entire house.

This left me in difficulties. The baby was heavier than I expected and made up of parts that defied my best efforts to contain. First a plump leg shot free of the blanket and then, no sooner had managed to cover it, than a stubbornly clenched fist appeared. I did not like to make too much fuss for fear of waking the child, whose wrinkled features and smooth skin brought to mind another situation like this many years ago.

"This is how you used to look when you were asleep," I reminisced to my sibling. "Everyone said you were a beautiful baby."

Sherlock was unmoved.

"A pity they never saw you when you were awake. You cried constantly. You were a miserable little wretch. In fact, brother," I said, ignoring his scowl, "you still are. And I do wish you wouldn't talk like that about marriage in front of our cousins. I care to think that we at least are a beacon of normality, however faint, despite the unhappy circumstances of our ancestry."

"I am here under sufferance, Mycroft," said he loftily. "Of all the places, I would choose to be this afternoon, Finchley is not one of them. I would rather face the vilest criminal in London than have to endure Cousin Esme's attentions. If I was blunt, it was because I judged it better not to pander to her delusions. Indifference seems only to encourage her, although, knowing Esme, I daresay that my curtness will only stiffen her resolve."

"Nevertheless, do try to be amenable. This is a christening, not a funeral. I have yet to hear you congratulate Masterman or his dear wife. It is the done thing, you know. And my godson is a most handsome child. Don't you agree?"

He nodded grudgingly. "Their choice of name was unfortunate, however."

"Wenceslaus Randle Enoch Nicholas Carey Holmes? No, I cannot agree with you there, Sherlock. It is a trifle long perhaps."

"I was thinking of his initials, Mycroft. 'Wrench' is unusual even in our family."

"Not necessarily. Had Father had his way, he would have named you Aloysius Sherlock Holmes. Your initials would have been that of a popular woodland tree."

"I am obliged to whomsoever brought him to his senses. As for this child, whatever possessed Masterman to choose such a name as Wenceslaus?"

Unfortunately, this rather pertinent remark was made in a voice loud enough in the sudden silence that accompanied Esme's return to be overheard by the mother's family. Masterman's stony-faced mother-in-law advanced like a ship in full sail, all billowing shawls and tight rigging.

"Wenceslaus was my late father's name, sir," said she, her fixed scowl never breaking for an instant. "We haven't been introduced, not surprisingly since my son-in-law is noticeably lacking in the social graces. I am Mrs Goddard, the grandmother of this child. You are?"

"Mycroft Holmes at your service, madam. This is my younger brother, Sherlock."

"I daresay he is," said she, looking him up and down with the sort of expression one reserves for inspecting threadbare rugs presented as prized antiques. "And what is it you do?"

When he told her, thankfully omitting to call it a trade, she grimaced slightly.

"Our neighbours were visited by a detective once," said she with distaste. "We never spoke to them again after that."

"I trust they were not too inconvenienced by the loss of your company," said Sherlock.

She gave him a strange look, as though undecided whether

60

his remark was intended to be offensive or not.

"You work in government, I understand," she said, addressing me. "My late father always called it an institution for scoundrels."

"Then his intelligence was beyond question," said my brother.

"I am told that the present administration is likely to lose power at the next election," Mrs Goddard went on. "Have you made provision for that eventuality, Mr Holmes?"

"In what respect?"

"Why, to protect your godchild from the disgrace, of course." She appeared surprised that such a thought had not already occurred to me. "To suffer the indignity of having one's godparent fallen so low is a great weight for such young shoulders." She sniffed dismissively. "I am surprised that my son-in-law asked you, knowing your situation. My own dear brother would have been a better choice. He's a clergyman, you know. The Bishop thinks very highly of him."

"But not enough to give him his own parish," said Sherlock, surveying the man with that critical eye of his. "Or should I say, to trust him with another flock. Was it drink that led to his fall from grace the last time, or was it a woman? I could not help but notice from the way that he has one hand around my Cousin Daisy's waist and the other clasped about his brandy glass that he is overly familiar and more than comfortable with both."

Mrs Goddard looked thunderstruck. Her mouth moved up and down, and yet the only words she could manage came out as so much nonsense. Finally she said something about needing some fresh air and excused herself, much to my brother's amusement.

"I fear you have not helped Masterman's cause," I said solemnly. "Was that necessary?"

"Honesty in all things, Mycroft."

"Undoubtedly. But there is a time and a place for everything. Good heavens, if this is how you disport yourself in company, it is no wonder that you have yet to make your mark."

"Would you have had me lie and sing the praises of an inebriated libertine over my own brother? As for that odious woman, is there any truth in what she said? Might you lose your position at Whitehall?"

"It is possible. Nothing is certain."

"How inconvenient for you. How will you live?"

"I shall have to manage as best I can. The real question is, Sherlock, how will you manage?"

This consideration did not seem to trouble him in the slightest. "I shall live by my wits," he declared. "Failing that, I shall come to lodge with you."

"Most certainly you will not!"

"Oh? Would you see me turned out onto the streets? Would you have me play my violin on street corners and—" He stopped short and his nose wrinkled. "What *is* that appalling smell?"

Now he mentioned it, a curiously unpleasant odour had arisen from somewhere. In my arms, the baby began to writhe and his tiny face creased into an unhappy frown. His crying brought his mother hurrying to our side and there was much talk about having the maid attend to his needs.

I am not wholly ignorant as to the meaning of such things, although I would rather it had not occurred whilst I had been holding him. Even when the child was removed, a faint aroma lingered, as though it had imprinted itself on the delicate lining of my nose and refused to be shifted even after liberal quantities of snuff. What with that and the smell of the fish, I was beginning to feel quite faint. When hostilities again broke out between Tollemarche and Clarence, the one ending up with his face in the salad bowl and the other being pelted with hard boiled eggs, it seemed like the ideal opportunity to make our excuses and leave.

None of us covered ourselves in glory that afternoon – our cousins opted for custard, cream and lettuce instead – and my abiding memory will ever be of the look on Mrs Goddard's face when a pork pie sailed through the air and exploded in a mass of jelly and fatty meat in her lap.

All I can say is that if that is the worst that ever happens to her at one of our family gatherings, then she may consider herself fortunate for having got off so lightly. Stranger things than flying pies have happened before now.

Monday, 8ᵗʰ March, 1880

It has happened.

The enfranchised have spoken – or at least those who could be bothered to turn out did, and in so doing have exercised their right to decide for the apathetic voter and everyone else alike who shall be responsible for the governance of this nation.

The result of this underwhelming outpouring of enthusiasm for the political system and its democratic workings is that we are to have a change of government.

On such occasions one feels obliged not to desert the sinking ship until the last of the timbers have disappeared from sight. The news began to dribble in towards the late afternoon, picking up momentum at supper time and reaching torrential levels by early evening. No one was much surprised by the ways things were headed. Indeed, in certain quarters, I am led to understand that there was relief that the burden of public resentment and hostility should be passed onto younger shoulders.

This feeling was not universal, for I found one poor fellow crying his eyes out on the stairs, declaring that now he had lost his seat, he would have to go home and make conversation with his wife, with whom he had not passed three hours since Easter last. I advised him to find himself a hobby that would take him out of the house for long periods of time. He muttered something about long walks, which I would have thought would have been preferable under the circumstances, as long as said spouse was uninterested in dirtying her shoes on good country soil.

All of this is of little immediate interest to me, having neither a seat to lose nor a seat to win. What does concern me, however, is my future.

Evidently this was praying on the mind of others, for mid-afternoon an unhappy group of civil servants descended on me and asked for my opinion of their prospects.

"I hear they intend to cut back on the staff," said their leader, a sharp-eyed, sharp-nosed Principal Private Secretary by the name of Sneers – an apt appellation considering the amount of sneering he does – repeating a rumour that tends to do the rounds at every change of government. "It's all very well you acting blasé, Holmes, but there's only so many accountants needed around here."

This, I gathered, was aimed at me, although it hit its mark in another of the party, a thin, balding fellow, with a permanently-worried expression graven deep into the lines of his face. On hearing this, he let out a groan and bewailed the fate of his wife and three small children.

His reaction was perhaps justified. The practice in recent years has been towards packing the offices with as many people as possible, so that one is obliged to do battle with one's colleagues for a chair, as there are never enough to go round. This conspicuous policy of full employment, we are told, was done to inspire confidence, following that old adage that no one wants to do business with a company that appears to be in such difficulties that it can afford only a tea lady, office boy, and one aged clerk.

What Sneers does not know – what I daresay that many do not know – that accountancy forms but one small part of my daily activities, and that chiefly involves totting up my receipts for expenses and doing the Prime Minister's tax returns. This latter service has kept me in favour with the current administration, as last year I was able to save Lord Kettleby 2s.4d., for which he said he was eternally grateful. I do not doubt it, but eternal gratitude will be of little use to me now he is no longer in charge.

I do not deceive myself that omniscience and completing other people's tax returns are any guarantee of permanence. If I continue under Lord Kettleby's successor, I can foresee a situation where I would have to prove myself – and unlike our wailing friend, I do not have the luxury of claiming hardship for my family. Having a brother with an unusual occupation, who on occasion turns to me for financial support, does not produce the same feelings of charity as does the plight of a wife and three small children.

In the circumstances, however, since I am neither a diviner of the future nor privy to the intentions of the incoming administration, I could only advise the troubled band that we should all have to wait and see.

This did not satisfy Sneers, whose Parthian shot was that we were none of us indispensible, with the exception of himself. It was on the tip of my tongue to say that even Principal Private Secretaries had been known to lose their jobs before now when my attention was diverted by the arrival of a telegram from Cousin Masterman. My fear of bad news concerning my godson was allayed when on reading it I discovered that it concerned another of our family, namely Cousin Aubrey. The message read:

'As you value our reputation and the happiness of your

godson, please do not let Aubrey disgrace us.'

The last I had heard of Aubrey was what Masterman had himself told me at the christening. Our benighted cousin had chained himself to the railings at Waterloo as an act of protest, there to remain until the trains ceased to run or he found the key to his padlock, whichever came first. An account of events since then were to be found in the morning paper, where a half-column detailed the arrest of a Mr A. Holmes on a charge of criminal damage and theft of railway property.

According to the report, Aubrey had unbolted the section of railings to which he was chained and had been caught trying to leave the scene with said railings still attached to him. The poor devil must have got hungry and, with no sign of his missing keys, had been forced to take more drastic action.

I dislike intervening on behalf of family members who fall into folly through their own foolishness, but I did have some sympathy for Aubrey's plight. Had the police intervened sooner to release him, the situation would never have reached such an unedifying climax. One could understand, though not applaud their reasoning in leaving him where they knew he could not make a nuisance of himself, but clearly this attitude had driven him to these desperate measures.

I felt indignant on Aubrey's behalf for a good five minutes. That was quite long enough – any longer would have given me indigestion.

A more pressing concern was the spectacle he would make of himself if the case came to court. The timing of an embarrassment of this nature in view of the uncertainty of my position could not have been worse. Accordingly, I made a few discreet enquiries, called upon several favours and had Aubrey released quietly and without fuss by early evening.

By half past five, I decided I had shown loyalty enough to the outgoing administration for one night and resolved to wend my way home. So I should have done but for the sounds of sobbing I heard as I passed Mrs Bright's domain. Fearing that some disaster had overtaken her aunt and her beau at Worthing, I took the unwise step of investigating the matter further.

"It's this election, sir," she explained when I asked the cause of her distress. "It's upset me no end, I can tell you."

She made a show of dabbing at her eyes with her wet apron, prompting me to offer her my handkerchief instead. Her tears were dried, her nose was blown and then the article was handed back to me. I declined, as a gentleman should, with grace and protestations that the lady should keep it in case she was overcome again.

"You are kind, Mr Holmes sir," said she. "That's what I like about working here. Everyone's been so good to me. And now they'll all have to leave. Oh, sir, what will become of all my poor gentleman?"

"I expect they will have to amuse themselves as best they can, Mrs Bright."

"I'm a silly old so-and-so," said she, smiling faintly, "but I shall miss them all, especially that nice gentleman, Sir Horace – one sugar and a dash of milk. Oh, I beg your pardon. I mean, the Assistant Under-Secretary – that's how I remember how he likes his tea, you see. And he's always been so good to me."

Not too good, I hoped, given the man's reputation with members of the opposite sex.

"And you, Mr Holmes, you've always had a kind word to say, especially when my aunt had her trouble. There's not many would have cared."

There was a concupiscent gleam in her eye as she spoke that put me on my guard. "As long as you are quite well, Mrs Bright," I said, deciding it was high time I was on my way. "I'm sure they will keep you on. Ministers may come and go, but a good cleaner is worth her weight in gold. I shall put in a good word for you, have no fear about that."

"They'll be keeping you on then, Mr Holmes?"

"I do not know. That depends on the decision of the next prime minister."

"Is he a nice man?"

"I cannot say, Mrs Bright. I have yet to meet him."

"You don't know how he takes his tea then? I ask because you can tell a lot about a man from the way he takes his tea."

"Can you really?"

"Oh, yes. Them who like the milk in first are always gamblers, on account of them taking a chance as to how strong the tea will be, you see. Then there's them who like to have the pot stirred before the tea is poured. There's not many of them working here, on account of them being the type of gentlemen who don't like to take risks. Them who don't take sugar should, because they often have bitter streaks, while them that do have the sweetest tempers." She smiled at me again. "Like you, Mr Holmes. You like your three sugars, don't you? There's some who'd say it was too sweet, but you always say 'just right', just like my old Edward."

"Do I?" I said, fumbling for the doorknob. "I'll have to watch that in future."

"He always used to like three sugars in his tea, God rest him," she sighed. "Have I ever told you that you remind me of him, sir? He was a big burly man too. And he loved his muffins he did. Do you like muffins, Mr Holmes? I'll make some just for you. They'd go down a treat with your three o'clock tomorrow."

"Really, Mrs Bright," I said, "do not put yourself to any trouble on my account."

"It's no trouble at all, Mr Holmes," she purred. "It's nice to have a man about the place who appreciates my cooking."

The doorknob finally turned, and I was able to stagger back through the open door and away from her clutches.

Unfortunately, my hasty departure caused me to collide with the solid figure of the Assistant Under-Secretary, who grumbled something about my stepping on his corns.

"Confound it all, you clumsy fool!" said Sir Horace. "What do you think you are doing, hurling yourself out of doorways like that?"

"I was talking to Mrs Bright."

"And don't you worry about your three o'clock, Mr Holmes," the wretched woman said as she passed us carrying her mop and bucket. "I'll see you're well looked after."

The Assistant Under-Secretary narrowed his eyes. "You scoundrel, sir!"

"She meant muffins," I said in vain.

"Muffins be damned! By George, if I were a younger man, I'd take you outside and give you a proper thrashing. There's no place for dalliers here at Whitehall, or muffins come to that. If there's any dallying to be done, I'll be doing it. We've had enough trouble getting decent staff as it is without young puppies like you upsetting the apple cart." He rose up on his toes and looked at me down the length of his not inconsiderable nose. "Do we understand each other, Holmes?"

"Not entirely, Sir Horace," I replied, thoroughly vexed by the man and his bad breath. "We appear to be talking at cross purposes. Furthermore, if you want muffins with your tea, sir, I should direct your request to Mrs Bright. I'm sure she would be happy to oblige. She appreciates a man with a healthy appetite, especially if he takes three sugars in his tea."

And with that I took my leave. I have long been of the opinion that the Assistant Under-Secretary is quite deranged, a quality that made his choice of a career in government inevitable. I half expected to hear his footsteps behind me at every turn and it was not until I was in the inner sanctum of my club that I was able to breathe easy again.

Friday, 12th March, 1880

Given my encounter with the Assistant Under-Secretary on Monday, I had endeavoured for the better part of the past week to stay out of the way of both Sir Horace and Mrs Bright with her homemade offerings. I am not entirely ignorant of how these things work: what starts with Victoria Sandwich and muffins invariably progresses to toast and jam and sardine sandwiches, and before a fellow knows it, he is knee-deep in bills, children and the complexities of home plumbing.

Moreover, on those rare occasions when I did return to my office, it was to the whispers and sly glances of the junior clerks; as usual, the Whitehall gossipers had been hard at work, a welcome diversion, I should say, after this tiresome talk of elections and pending unemployment.

Today, however, my good fortune ran out. Quite by accident I was at my desk when Mrs Bright came round, a good twelve minutes later than usual.

The thing one could always say about Mrs Bright was that she was always punctual. Her tea might have been stewed, her biscuits soggy, but her time-keeping was impeccable.

Her tardiness was, therefore, a matter of some note. Nor was this the only change in her. At first I thought she had done her hair differently, but the same regulation amount of pins were present as usual, holding the same curls in place atop her head. Indeed, if I may be so blunt – since this is my journal, I believe I am entitled to take that liberty – it was my observation that the lady fairly radiated happiness, in much the same way as a muddy hound fills a room with the odour of damp dog.

This irregularity in Mrs Bright's demeanour I was sure had nothing to do with me, and I was confirmed in this conviction when she hardly seemed to notice me at all. I was presented with a tepid cup of weak tea with four sugars and the most perfunctory of stirs, so that the last few mouthfuls were sweet enough to make my teeth ache. Best of all, I was back to biscuits, and broken ones at that.

My absence over the last few days has not, as the poets claim, made Mrs Bright's heart grow fonder. On the contrary, I should say that I have been replaced in the lady's affections by none other than the Assistant Under-Secretary. That he has taken to wearing a carnation in his buttonhole of the same hue and variety as those glimpsed by the post boy in Mrs Bright's private domain is conclusive, I should say.

This felicitous escape was made all the sweeter by the prospect of Dover sole for supper, a dish at which the chef at the club has proved himself more than capable.

I say 'capable' in the loosest sense, for his style of cookery is somewhat erratic. Ever since Sir Daghurst Jones remarked the day after we had employed the man that he had been indisposed for the better part of the night, our chef has lived in mortal fear of poisoning the members. Everything sent out of the kitchen is cooked to within an inch of edibility. As a result, the greens are invariably limp, the meat invariably tough and the gravy invariably burnt. One dares not ask for one's steak to be well done unless one wishes it to be cremated.

The one exception to this is Dover sole. Why that should be I cannot say. However, I do not wish to tempt fate by questioning our chef on the subject. Let sleeping dogs lie, I say.

This being the case, I should have enjoyed it, and would have done so but for the presence of Sherlock, who came at my invitation and proceeded to make himself disagreeable. That he turned up an hour late and then scarcely touched his food did not make him the best of dining companions. The black cloud he brought with him soon grew over our table, so that the meal was not as pleasurable as it should have been.

If I had asked the cause of this melancholic turn of his mood, I would have been regaled with a tale of woe regarding a want of ingenuity in the criminal fraternity. For that reason, I did not ask. The simple fact that Sherlock fails to grasp is that for those of us who regard the paucity of serious crime as a thing to be lauded, his lamentations on the subject are never likely to win him sympathy, except from someone with a similar thirst for reckless adventure and derring-do.

If such a fellow exists, I should like to meet him, if only to prove that my brother is not as peculiar in his interests as his inclinations might suggest. If I could go one further and introduce him to Sherlock, then they might go on their merry way and do their derring together – and spare me having to worry about my brother's entanglements with the baser side of human nature.

Dessert came and went, and I was turning my attention to something to settle the stomach when Sherlock surprised me by refusing a whisky.

"Are you unwell?" I asked, concerned now that what I had

taken for sullenness might have some medical cause.

"No," said he laconically.

"Do you dislike the club's choice of whisky?"

"No."

"Have you then forsworn the grain? I know many a man who prefers the grape."

"Mycroft," said he, finally stirred out of his monosyllabic ill humour, "what is the point of these questions?"

"I merely ask why you have developed an unreasonable aversion to whisky. Since you show a disdain for medical opinion and any claims made by advertisements—"

"A healthy degree of scepticism where the press is concerned is to be recommended."

"Quite so, my dear boy, quite so. If I believed half of what I read in the papers, I should have emigrated long ago. With regards to your problem, by a process of elimination, I should say it has something to do with one of those criminal investigations in which you persist in dabbling."

"I do not dabble, Mycroft," said he testily. "But if you must know, my sudden 'aversion' *is* connected with a case, currently my last and with no other in sight."

"As I thought. Well," I said when he seemed reluctant to impart the details, "we have come this far. You might as well tell me the rest of the sordid tale."

His expression settled somewhere between a frown and impudence, and he finally deigned to tell me more. "On Monday last, a wine merchant named Vamberry was found drowned in a barrel of imported whisky."

"And the sight of it stirs up memories of his unhappy death. I quite understand, Sherlock."

"No, it is not that," said he, with something approaching a sly gleam in his eyes. "It was hearing that his employees intended to bottle up what was left after the corpse was removed and put it

74

on general sale. They said something about their former employer having been thoughtful in the manner of his death for he had 'improved the flavour'."

I was sorry Sherlock had not mentioned this before, especially as I was halfway through my second whisky.

"Why were you consulted?" I asked, setting my glass aside.

"Because the circumstances of his death were deemed to be suspicious."

"Ah, he was murdered. It was the brother-in-law, of course."

Sherlock started from his chair. "How the deuce did you know that?"

As an elder sibling, few pleasures are bestowed upon me by virtue of my position, save those which I can elicit for myself. Sherlock fancies himself unique; indeed, he has twice the natural arrogance of an ordinary man of his intelligence and upbringing. Occasionally, I hold that it is my duty to prick the bubble of his self-importance and prove to him that Nature has not smiled on him alone. That he never fails to disappoint with his reaction is really quite delightful.

"The same way I know that he is an educated man, hard-working, but undervalued by his wife's family and resentful because of it," I explained, warming to my subject. "Come now, sir, do not look so surprised. The manner of the man's death suggested the possibility immediately. It was George, Duke of Clarence, who was drowned in a vat of Malmsey wine in the Tower of London, so the Bard of Warwick would have us believe, on the orders of his brother, King Edward IV, against whom he had been in revolt."

Sherlock looked perplexed and dissatisfied by my explanation. Naturally, I felt compelled to further enlighten him.

"The similarity struck me at once. Historical precedent has

much to teach us, Sherlock. That the brother-in-law knew of the incident tells us that he is a man of erudition. I imagine that Vamberry's own brother was very much in the mould of the 'prodigal son', welcomed back into the fold with open arms and promise of advancement in the family business over the heads of those who had toiled without complaint and were more deserving. How am I doing thus far?"

"You are correct on every count," he conceded.

"With the prospect of the business falling into the hands of an ingrate and a wastrel, the brother-in-law felt compelled to take action to protect his interests. Killing the returning brother would not do; I daresay he thought this man Vamberry could not be trusted to repeat this act of disloyalty with another member of the family. Vamberry had to die and the brother was to be blamed. The man's business and the historical connotations suggested to him the manner of how the crime was to be achieved. That is where the fellow made his mistake. Had he hit Vamberry over the head and left it at that, the identity of the murderer might never have been questioned. But death by whisky – how very dramatic, not to mention a waste of good spirits. Beware the crime that is too obvious, Sherlock."

I was pleased with my efforts, although Sherlock was rather less so. That I had done so from the comfort of my chair seemed to vex him, when, as he explained, he had had to follow a more strenuous line of investigation. When I put it to him that a little more thought and a little less action might be in order in the future, his mood deteriorated to such an extent that he saw fit to make an implausible excuse about having to see a man about a dog and promptly left.

Like that old monarch, King Lear, I was the pattern of all patience, and said nothing about this want of manners. No one ever said that an elder brother's lot was destined to be an easy one, after all.

Saturday, 13ᵗʰ March, 1880

Loath as I am to believe anything Sherlock tells me – I have been accustomed to treating all and any information gathered from that quarter without the use of thumbscrews or a threat to cut off his allowance with caution – in light of today's events, I find that I may be compelled to revise that opinion or, at the very least, to subject all further offerings to a good deal more scrutiny.

I note from yesterday's journal entry that last night he told he had 'to see a man about a dog'. This I understand from certain well-informed sources, namely our hall porter, has a meaning pertaining to what our dear departed father would have called 'life's necessities'.

I can remember this phrase of his perplexing us for the longest time. 'Life's necessities' by Father's definition depended on what happened to be a necessity at any given moment. Over time, it came to include everything from putting on one's stockings to playing billiards. By the time he shrugged off this mortal coil, his daily routine was entirely devoted to the call of 'life's necessities' to the exclusion of anything else. One can only conclude that he died of sheer exhaustion.

Returning to my brother, when he made this passing allusion, I had no reason to suppose it was anything other than the lamentable result of his having frequented too many low drinking establishments where one might hear that sort of thing bandied about quite openly as if it were a subject worthy of debate. I thought at the time that it showed a want of decorum, and I had quite made up my mind to take my wayward sibling to task over what I perceived to be a lapse in his judgement.

My opportunity came in the afternoon when Sherlock invaded my inner sanctum, as I call my private chamber at the club, where I was going through the accounts and discovering to my dismay that the petty cash was short by a shilling. I was not expecting him – so I should have been on my guard, for that is usually the time he appears – and as a consequence was somewhat taken aback when he burst into the room without having the good grace to knock first. His disagreeable temper of the night before had left him, and his mood was what I should describe as conspiratorial. From this, I deduced that he wanted something.

"Mycroft, are you busy?" said he.

The papers spread out across my desk should have told him that without having to ask.

"I am in need of a favour."

It was as I suspected. I adopted my usual expression of tolerant fraternal benevolence and sat back in my chair with my fingers pressed together in that superior manner beloved by bank managers before they announce that one's account is overdrawn and further credit is to be denied.

"How much is it this time?"

"Nothing as base as money," said he, sniffing disdainfully.

78

I do wish he would not say that sort of thing. Money, whether in want or excess, may indeed have a great deal for which to answer, but it does at least deserve respect. Only those who have wealth in abundance can afford to sneer at it, and even then they do so at their peril. We had an uncle once who was fond of declaring that the money in his pocket was not worth the paper it was printed on, so much so that the police decided to take him at his word and found that he had been printing his own currency in defiance of the Bank of England.

"I was wondering," he went on innocently, "if you could look after something for me for a few hours."

I had been curious as to what part the ungainly lump I could see bundled inside his coat was to play in this drama. In my ignorance, I imagined it to be fairly innocuous.

"Very well," I said, returning to my books. "Leave it in the corner out of the way."

"I shall try. I'm not sure he will stay there."

"Who won't?"

Who, or rather what, proved to be the ugliest looking mongrel I have seen for many a year. The result of an ill-starred match between a lurcher and a spaniel, it had one blue eye, one brown, both set wide apart along a long, scarred nose, whilst its drooping ears were ragged and uneven. It resembled a child's first needlework experiment gone wrong, hastily cobbled together with odd bits and pieces of fabric to create something that was a close approximation to what someone who had never seen a dog imagined how one might look.

It was a panting, drooling, whining, struggling, excitable mess of a creature. Worst of all, it appeared to be devoted to my brother, for when it was not clambering all over him, it was licking his face.

"What on earth is that?" I said.

"It's a dog, Mycroft."

"Evidently it is a dog. What is it doing here? We have a no-dog rule at the Diogenes."

This is in accordance with the other clubs with which we share Pall Mall. It is the one rule, aside from smoking and spitting out of the club windows, that generates the most complaints from our members. It is strange to note how many of them have asked at one time or another to allow entrance for their canine companions, and yet none of them have asked the same for their wives.

"I cannot take him home with me," Sherlock continued, "so I was hoping—"

"Certainly not!" I declared. "This is a gentlemen's club, not a kennel."

"He'll be no trouble." The dog panted and whined and struggled in his arms. "You are a good boy, aren't you, Toby?"

The fact that the animal had a name suggested a worrying possibility. "Am I to take it, Sherlock, that this creature belongs to you?"

"Indirectly," said he, fending off the slavering tongue. "I found him when he was a pup. An acquaintance looks after him for me. I borrow him from time to time when I need help with an investigation."

It did not have the look of a guard dog, unless it apprehended suspects by bowling them to the ground and slobbering over them until they could be arrested by the proper authorities.

"He has a quite remarkable nose," Sherlock elaborated. "Give him a scent and he will follow it half across London."

"And the other half?"

"No one is infallible, Mycroft. Toby himself has an eye for the ladies, which has led to his disgrace more times than I care to remember. It will be the ruin of him one day, mark my words." This was directed at the loyal creature, in a tone of voice that

80

suggested he was not as firm in reproving its moral lapses as he might have been. "It is Toby's predilection in that direction that has resulted in our current predicament. There was an incident recently with a prize poodle that has led to its owner threatening violence against him and a suit against me. Mr Sherman, who has care of him, informed me yesterday that the lady's agent has been making enquiries about Toby's whereabouts with a view to some mischief, and so we decided that it would be safer for Toby to be out of the vicinity until the excitement has died down."

I knew where this was leading and pre-empted the coming request with a flat refusal. "He cannot stay here, Sherlock."

"He cannot stay with me either. I smuggled him into my rooms last night, but I fear my landlady was suspicious. She asked if I had heard a dog barking. I had to blame it on a cough. I cannot repeat the exercise tonight or she will think I am ailing and turn me out."

"Well, then, there is a home for lost dogs in Battersea[5]. Take him there."

"I never thought you so callous, Mycroft. Look at his face," said he, turning the grizzled muzzle in my direction. "Do you not see intelligence there?"

What I saw was shedding hairs and copious amounts of saliva dripping from the quivering tongue onto the club's antique Turkish rug. Granted, there was something appealing about the large eyes and the slightly comical turn of the mouth, but as a rule, I am not sentimental over animals.

If I set aside all other considerations, however, I was left with the fact that this ungainly creature had seen fit to adopt my brother and bestow upon him his unquestioning loyalty. I have ever tried to be accommodating to Sherlock's friends in the past,

---

[5] Battersea Dogs & Cats Home was initially established in Holloway in as the 'Temporary Home for Lost and Starving Dogs'. The Home moved to Battersea in 1871.

although they have been few and far between, and to refuse one now, on the grounds of my personal feelings towards the animal, would be uncharitable on my part.

Accordingly, I relented and tried to be gracious in defeat.

"Splendid!" said Sherlock, unleashing the hound, which, freed of restraint, took several turns around the room at speed, scratching the parquet floor with its claws and splattering the walls with drool, before coming to rest at my side. It stared up me, its oddly-coloured eyes large and liquid in that manner calculated to reduce the hardest-hearted fellow to tears.

"It will only be for a few hours, until I can make alternative arrangements."

"Make sure it is," I said. "If you haven't returned by five, I shall deliver him to the nearest policeman as a stray."

He departed, making the usual promises that he would return long before the appointed hour, and I was left with my curious companion. I could not work; every time I chanced to look down, it was to find the dog still staring up at me. Every time I caught his eye, something rose in his expression that was too much like eagerness. The brows lifted, the panting became frenzied and he tapped his paws in readiness for the chase.

I fear I disappointed him one too many times, for finally he took himself away and wandered in a desultory fashion about the room, sniffing and investigating every nook and cranny.

When silence descended and he was gone out of my sight for too long, I fretted about what mischief he might be perpetrating. Not having him at my side was infinitely worse than having him there. When he did emerge into view, it was with lowered head, sloping shoulders and drooping tail, coupled with the most mournful expression ever worn by human or canine alike.

With nothing to do, he gravitated back to my desk and presently laid himself across my feet, a warm and heavy, though not displeasing, presence that gave off gentle snores coupled with the occasional muttered 'woof' to mark the progress of his dreams.

So we spent the rest of the afternoon. Five came and went, and by half past six it was evident that my brother had abandoned us both to our own devices. I was feeling tired and hungry, since I had been unwilling to leave the dog alone with my paperwork while I dined downstairs. I had a meal of rabbit and ham-hock brought up, at which point Toby stirred and planted himself at my side again. I tried to ignore him, but the whine was persistent and he adopted a begging posture on his hind legs that proved fatal to my resolve.

We shared the meal after that, with the result that neither of us was satisfied with our portions. I had to send down to the kitchen to request something else, and was presented with gammon, cold chicken, a hard-boiled egg and an enquiry from the chef whether I had found his meal at fault. Not at all, I replied; I was particularly hungry and had that night a taste for meat. The obliging man then sent up every last scrap of beef, mutton and pork he could find, and Toby dined royally.

By eight, it was evident that I would have to carry out my threat in the absence of Sherlock and hand Toby over to the police. This seemed hard on the dog, but a greater principle was at stake. My brother had to learn that he could not impose on the charity of other people and not expect them to feel aggrieved when he failed to keep his side of the arrangement.

Accordingly, I found Toby's leash and we went out together by the club's back door lest the dog's presence be discovered and my continued membership be called into question.

I cannot say how many times we walked the length of Pall Mall in search of a constable. That is frequently the way of these things. One can never find a policeman when one is needed, but should one commit some minor indiscretion, one may expect to feel a hand on one's collar without delay. As it was, after half an hour, I had had more exercise in one night than I might reasonably expect to undertake in a month and Toby was becoming fractious. I did not blame him; we were both victims of Sherlock's appalling lack of consideration. Indeed, I hold my brother entirely responsible for the events that followed.

We were at the St James's end of Pall Mall, I still looking for a constable and Toby attending to 'life's necessities' when I heard someone clearing their throat behind me in an authoritative manner. I turned to find the object of my search, a large, solid-looking fellow with a deceptively-placid visage and deep-set eyes agleam with suspicion.

"Good evening, sir," said he. "Do you mind telling me what you're doing?"

"As a matter of fact, Constable, I have been looking for you."

"Looking for me? Now why's that, sir? I don't think I know you, do I?"

He said it in that slightly sardonic manner beloved by anyone in authority when they know you are in no position to retort with a witty remark.

"I've been watching you for a while now," he went on. "You've been up and down this road several times. I'd call that suspicious behaviour, wouldn't you?"

"I would say it depends on one's individual circumstances," I said vaguely.

"I daresay it does, but we've had reports of someone matching your description making a nuisance of himself by knocking on doors and running away." He looked me up and down. "That wouldn't be you by any chance, sir?"

It crossed my mind that he could well be trying to test my patience. Certainly I found his question offensive. Did I look like the sort of man given to knocking on strangers' doors, to say nothing of being able to run away before they answered?

"Certainly not. As I say, I've been looking for a policeman."

"Now you've found one. What's your problem?"

"Well, it's this dog…"

I trailed off as we both looked down to find that Toby was busily watering the constable's trouser leg. If he seemed to find it amusing, the constable was less pleased.

"I see," said he, stoically. "Are you aware of the penalty for allowing your dog to foul a uniform belonging to a member of the Metropolitan Police?"

"No, what is it?"

He pursed his lips and considered. "I can't remember off-hand, but I'm sure it's very severe."

"Really, Constable, I do apologise," I stammered. "I do not know why he did it."

"Don't you now?" said he, taking a notebook out of his pocket and licking his pencil in readiness. "Well, I'd better have a name for my report."

"Toby."

"*Your* name, sir, not his. We can't summons a dog."

"Oh, Holmes. Mycroft Holmes."

"And this animal belongs to you, does it, Mr Holmes?"

"No, it is my brother's dog."

"His name is?"

"Mr Sherlock Holmes."

He paused in writing. "You're his brother?"

"Oh, you know him, do you?"

"Yes, sir, I'm afraid I do," said he with a weary sigh as he closed his notebook. "Makes a regular nuisance of himself down at headquarters, although I daresay he means well." He peered at me a little closer. "If you don't mind me saying, you don't look like him."

I shrugged helplessly.

"Well, we'll leave it at that, Mr Holmes. I daresay it was an accident and there's no harm done this time." He shook his leg and grimaced. "Mind you keep that dog under control in the future."

"Yes, Constable, I shall."

"You'd better get yourself off home now. The thieves will be out soon. Good evening, sir."

Doubtless it was good advice. The problem was that I was left with finding lodgings for Toby for the night. The police had let me down – or perhaps the dog had been hoping for that outcome all along; I was not entirely deceived by that winsome look of his – and so I had no other alternative but to take him home with me.

I adopted Sherlock's strategy of smuggling him in under my coat and, despite an anxious moment when my landlady came out of her room with a broom and wished me good night, we made it safely and undetected into my chambers. Once there, we stood looking at each other for a goodly while, trying to decide what to do with each other.

I settled for tying his leash to the leg of a chair and giving him an old blanket in the corner. This did not sit well with him, and for a long time whilst I warmed my aching feet before the fire I was aware of his plaintive whines and fretting behind me until he resigned himself to his lot.

Whether it was the warmth, the brandy or my choice of literature, I fell asleep in the chair and awoke some hours later when the church bells were chiming a quarter past two. The fire had died down and yet I was curiously warm. On investigation, it was to find that Toby's head was in my lap and his back was to the fire. Somehow he had succeeded not in freeing himself but in dragging the chair over to a more advantageous position. Enterprise deserves reward and so I left him asleep on the hearth rug whilst I took myself to my bed.

Come the morrow I shall locate that brother of mine – and give him a piece of my mind. If this is how he disports himself, I consider myself fortunate that the constable did not arrest both Toby and me on the basis of our association alone.

Sunday, 14ᵗʰ March, 1880

Today being Sunday, I assumed, mistakenly as it transpired, that this was to be my day of rest. I had not bargained for the machinations of Sherlock and his flea-ridden mongrel.

I am not my brother's dog's keeper, and I was determined, therefore, as soon as was decently possible, to return the creature from whence it came, namely to Sherlock's care. What he did with it after that was not my concern; with better training and a sterner hand on the leash, the dog would never have tarnished his reputation with the female members of his own species and their owners in the first place.

My idea of a decent hour was not Toby's. Bad enough that he had kept me awake most of the night with his stentorian snoring, restless prowling and annoying desire to curl up beside me on the bed, but when I did finally get off to sleep, I was jolted from my dreams at half past five by the sound of mournful howling. Much to my consternation, the dog had taken up position by the door and was lamenting of his woes in as loud a voice as he could muster.

This was a problem for me, for the terms of my tenancy specifically excluded the keeping of pets. The presence of a dog would not be welcomed by either Madame Fluffy or her owner, Mrs Creswell.

In somewhat of a panic, for I heard a thump from above, warning me that others were alert to Toby's dawn chorus and were coming to investigate, I was up and out of my bed before the remnants of sleep had cleared from my befuddled mind. I thrust my feet into my slippers, only to feel a warm liquid ooze up between my bare toes.

I did not have to look far for the culprit. Toby had stopped his howling and was gazing at me with his ears pricked and his head crooked on one side. He was the picture of innocence, and the expression he wore suggested his bewilderment as to what all the fuss was about. I did not blame the dog for following his nature. But I did blame my brother – and the cost of a new pair of slippers would be coming out of his allowance.

My wet feet aside, my immediate concern was silencing Toby. I must confess that I have not had many dealings with dogs. Our dear mother had a lap dog, a brown and white spaniel, which accompanied her everywhere until the day it died, whereupon she had it skinned and made into a lap rug. For many years it lay either across her knees or before the hearth, its glassy eyes forever fixed devotedly on its former owner, and we were expected to greet it and pat it on the head as if it lived and breathed still. An elderly great-aunt called it 'macabre', which, coming from a woman whose husband collected stuffed birds, I always thought rather ungenerous.

Only moths brought an end to its exalted tenure, and then it was packed away with instructions that it was to be placed in our mother's coffin to be buried with her. At this, our dear father had protested most vigorously, explaining that it would scandalise the vicar and upset the neighbours. Mother – always a practical soul – had said that she would be beyond caring what the neighbours or the vicar thought. Father then retaliated by saying that if she was to have her way, then he wanted to be buried with his *Racing Calendar* subscription grasped in his hand, lest any ne'er-do-well try to make free with any copies still owing to him.

Needless to say, both got their way. I believe no one was sorry to see the last of the dog-rug, but we did have several handsome offers for Father's subscription and something of a bidding war had broken out even as the undertaker was nailing down the coffin lid. Some said it was the way he would have wanted to go; speaking for myself, I thought it robbed the occasion of the dignity such a solemn undertaking demands.

However, I digress. I mention it only in relation to my current problem in misunderstanding the needs of a lithe and exuberant living dog. It pranced around my legs a good deal, near tripping me up, and whined and panted. This I took to mean that it wanted water, and took up a bowl with the object of filling it from the tap.

Unbeknown to me, Toby had other ideas. No sooner had I opened the door than the dog sprang through it and raced away. From downstairs came the frightened meow of a cat disturbed from its slumbers by a boisterous dog. This was then followed by the sort of noise one might easily have mistaken for the onward march of the hellish hordes as they thundered through the house. Mrs Creswell began to wail about a 'demon dog' rampaging through the house and the last I saw of Toby was his straggly tail vanishing through the front door as my landlady flung it open in an attempt to save her beloved Mrs Fluffy.

I returned quietly to my bed after that. The road outside was empty, and it was to be hoped that Toby was proving his worth in tracking down my absent brother. Even with the dog gone, my longed-for sleep was proving strangely elusive and so after several hours tossing and turning, I dressed with the intention of spending the day at my club. Just as I had finished my ablutions, Mrs Creswell knocked on my door to inform me that there was a policeman downstairs asking after me.

I agonised for several minutes that the nature of his visit concerned my brother and any number of potentially unhappy reasons for his failure to return the previous evening. My concern soon turned to dismay, however, when I saw it was the constable from the night before. In his hand he held a piece of string which was attached to Toby's collar.

"I believe this belongs to you," said he, holding out the impromptu leash to me.

I was aware of Mrs Creswell's lingering presence at my back and so stepped out into the street, closing the door behind me.

"As I explained last night, Constable," said I, "the dog belongs to my brother."

"He was in your care, sir."

"Until the moment it bolted out of this establishment and chose to desert me, yes, he was. After that, he acted on his own responsibility."

The constable gave one of those long, well-considered sniffs that gurgles in the nostrils and finally rattles its way to the back of the throat with unpleasant effect. Minor officials have to be able to master this before they are allowed to have any dealings with the general public, for they are told it adds an air of authority, whether real or imagined. In this case it was real, for the constable had taken out his notebook and was busy consulting it.

"Are you aware, Mr Holmes, that it is an offence to allow your dog to run loose or mad on the streets unattended?"

"It is not my dog," I repeated. I was growing weary of this conversation and, moreover, I was painfully aware that I was missing breakfast at the club. Being late is never recommended, for Sir Gervase Curdsley-Whey has acquired a reputation for devouring kippers in a manner which would put a denizen of the deep to shame. I saw my breakfast withering away to nothing whilst I bandied words with an officious policeman.

"It is classed as a nuisance, Mr Holmes, and as such it is my duty to summarily suppress such activities when appealed to do so by a member of the public. Having duly caught the animal, I now return it to you."

He held out the leash. Reluctantly, I took it.

"Furthermore, it is my duty to inform you that such negligence will incur a fine of five shillings, sir."

I handed the leash back to him. "Then you had best see my brother about that."

At this, to my satisfaction, he was somewhat taken aback and expressed his dismay by fixing upon me his official stare of disapproval, the one he reserved especially for mischievous small boys and recalcitrant dog owners.

"Am I to understand that you are refusing to take responsibility for the animal?" said he, licking his pencil in readiness to record my misdemeanours in his notebook. "I should inform you, sir, that too is an offence."

"On the contrary, I am not refusing. I am directing you to contact the owner of the animal. Whatever the dog has done is nothing to do with me."

The constable's frown deepened. "You know, sir, I've had dealings with some rum coves in my time, but none what would turn an animal from their door as callously as that. I've seen hardened criminals who've thought more of their cat than their fellow human beings, and yet here you are, a gentleman by all accounts, denying one of the Lord's innocent creatures." He shook his head sadly. "I never thought I'd live to see the day, but there, you get to meet all sorts in this job."

I did not care for the way I had been made to appear the villain of the piece. Even Toby seemed to hold it against me, for he whined, put his head upon his paws and stared up at me with those large, reproachful eyes of his, the very picture of canine misery.

"Well, there's nothing for it," the constable went on. "I'll have to take him into custody until the rightful owner comes forward and pays the fine."

"Better yet, why don't you return him to my brother?"

He rose up to his full height and glared at me down the length of his nose. "The Metropolitan Police Force has more important calls upon its time than tracing missing owners. If Mr Holmes wants his dog back, he'll have to come and get him. And if not…"

"Yes?" I enquired.

"Well, I might just keep him for myself," said he, stooping to pat Toby on the head. "I had a dog like this when I was a lad and the little 'uns are always pestering me to let them have a puppy."

I ventured that I thought this was a capital idea, earning myself the constable's further displeasure at what he considered my cavalier attitude. To my mind, the situation had worked to everyone's advantage. Toby was accompanying the constable to the King Street Police Station, where I had every confidence that he would be fussed over to his heart's content, and I was free to spend my Sunday in the usual fashion.

Without further delay, I took myself to the club, pausing only to instruct the hall porter to have the boy take a message to my brother, before hurrying to secure the last of the kippers from the greedy clutches of Sir Gervase. After that, I spent the better part of the day catching up on my sleep. By late afternoon, a

93

brewing storm had blown in a waif in the shape of Sherlock, who took it upon himself to lounge in the best chair before the fire and reprimand me for my shortcomings in respect to Toby.

"You said you would return to collect him yesterday," I reminded him.

"I was delayed, Mycroft," said he. "That was no reason to have Toby arrested."

"What nonsense, Sherlock." My brother does exaggerate so. It is a lamentable failing that a good education and years of study has only tended to encourage. "You have only to claim the animal to have him released."

"There I have encountered an obstacle. Constable Robbins, the arresting officer, said something about a fine."

"And the question of payment naturally arose. You have refused on principle?"

"Indeed, I have. The principle being that I have not five farthings to my name, let alone five shillings."

I should have expected as much. "Impecunious should have been your middle name. Whatever happened to the fee you collected from your involvement in that business with the wine merchant?"

He became unusually vague, as was his usual practice when he wanted to evade an awkward question.

"You did receive a fee?" I queried.

He made an airy gesture. "The money is not important, Mycroft. It was an intellectual exercise."

It was as I had expected. "Really, brother, this cannot continue. If you wish to continue to live in the manner to which you have become accustomed, you must overcome this natural diffidence of yours and broach the matter of payment. You cannot always rely upon me. This change of government has left me in an anomalous position, neither fish, flesh or... well, whatever the expression is."

"Good red herring, Mycroft," said he tartly. "And yet you have always told me that you are indispensible."

"I know it, but does the new administration? If I lose my position, what then shall become of us? Can I look to you to support me? I should be on my uppers before long if it came to that. What you need is a fixed scale of professional charges if you mean to continue in this venture. You cannot afford to work for nothing."

"A fixed scale of charges," he mused, "to hang upon my door like an advertisement in a shop window? I thought you disapproved of my dabbling in 'trade', as you called it."

"I would disapprove a good deal more if we both end our days in the workhouse."

"I shall give it some thought," said he dismissively. "As for Toby…"

I gave him the necessary money. "Have your dog released."

"That is most generous of you," said he, pocketing the money. "However, Constable Robbins and I have come to an understanding in that regard. Toby is to work off his debt to society in the constable's household by amusing the Robbins children until such time as it becomes safe for him to return to Mr Sherman's care. Overall, a very satisfactory arrangement for all concerned. Now, Mycroft, are you going to invite me to stay for dinner or am I to starve?"

Given this petty deceit and my loss of five shillings, to say nothing of my ruined slippers, leaving him to go hungry seemed like an excellent idea. Having the more charitable nature, however, I did relent on the subject of dinner, if only to deprive Sir Gervase of second and third helpings of the trout.

If I had hoped Sherlock would learn anything about responsibility from this business, I have been disappointed. My brother is almost feline in his ability to land on his feet no matter how disadvantageous the situation. It is a quality one might admire – that is, if one did not always find oneself inconvenienced by Sherlock's good fortune. And he still had the gall to expect dinner!

Monday, 26th April, 1880

I have been fretting about this day ever since the results of the last general election were released. Since the new administration took over, there has been a deathly hush over Whitehall. The axe has been falling, that much is certain. Mrs Bright has been walking the halls like a grim-eyed spectre, several accountants have been found crying on the stairs and the office cat has gone missing. The mood is not a happy one.

My own Judgement Day, as I have preferred to call it, started early with a summons to the Prime Minister's office at 9 o'clock. In a few days, change had already been effected. The charming country scene with a boy and his puppy that had always greeted the eye on entering the room had been replaced by a ship tossed on a tumultuous painted sea. I hoped that this was not a warning of things to come.

The new premier, Sir Piers Renfrew, a rangy, grey-haired man with deceptively benevolent eyes, was ensconced behind the desk with the natural grace of a man used to wielding authority. He left me in silence for a long time – a tactic to which I have become accustomed as a means of intimidating the weak and indecisive – before knitting his shaggy brows and leaning across the desk to peer at me.

"Holmes," he said slowly. "I knew an Aubrey Holmes once. Queer sort of chap. Saw him on the stage once, in the title role of Hamlet. Confounded fellow wouldn't die at the end! The stagehands had to come on and sit him down so the play could finish. Damnedest thing I ever saw." He grunted, though whether out of amusement or contempt I could not say. "Any relation of yours?"

"No, not at all," I said hastily. "I don't know the fellow."

Sir Piers stared hard at me. "Then why did you have him released from police custody after his arrest on a charge of criminal damage and theft of railway property a month or so ago?"

Evidently I had underestimated the man. The only course remaining to me was to tell the truth. "Yes," I admitted, "I'm sorry to say that he is a distant cousin of mine."

"Then why deny it? Be honest with me, sir, and you won't regret it. I can't abide a liar."

"Forgive me, sir, but if he was your cousin, would you?"

"Quite so, quite so," said he approvingly. "Well, I never judge a man by his relations. Got a few odd ones in the family myself, so I quite understand. What's this I hear about a brother?"

"My younger brother, Sherlock, sir. He's..." I struggled for words. "Harmless."

"I hear he's something of an amateur detective."

"You hear correctly, sir."

"Well, I never. Enterprising young fellow. I applaud

initiative. We need people with brains in this country." He sat back in his chair and steepled his fingertips. "Now, sir, what about you? I have had a good report about you from my predecessor. Reading between the lines, it seems to me that you're a jack-of-all-trades. But tell me, are you master of none?"

"It is true that I have a broad range of expertise, Prime Minister."

"Ah, then you imagine yourself to be one of those clever fellows, eh? In my experience, a know-all knows nothing but theories and therefore nothing of practical value. I suppose you can tell me at the drop of a hat what the square root of 2,598,681 is?"

As it so happened, I could. "1,612.04, sir."

"Is it?" He seemed taken aback. "As I say, interesting, but of little use to me, Mr…" He hesitated and squinted at the written sheet on the desk before him. "Damn secretary of mine writes like a drunken spider. What's this first name of yours?"

"Mycroft, sir."

"No, no, your name, not where you live."

"No, Prime Minister, my name is Mycroft."

His brows furrowed. "Queer sort of name. Still, I knew a fellow once name of Humble, who was anything but. Well now, Mr Mycroft Holmes, are you partisan or are you marzipan?"

It is not something to which I have ever given much thought. Our dear father was a staunch Tory, for no better reason than that his father had been one before him. In fine family tradition, he expected his two sons to follow suit, only to be disappointed when neither of us showed any particular inclination either way, having disdain enough and little regard for both.

For myself, my position forbids the luxury of political bias. As for being 'marzipan', I have been called many things in my time – the worst perhaps being an 'opinionist' and this from my own brother – but never have I been compared to a compound of almonds and sugar. On balance, however, I decided it was the lesser of the two evils.

"Marzipan?" I ventured uncertainly.

Sir Piers beamed. "Capital, capital. That means you can be moulded. There's no room for small minds in this administration. No room for small waists either." He appraised me with a critical eye. "You're a fellow of considerable girth, Holmes, I see. I admire a man who wears his vices openly, and believe me, gluttony is the one vice it is impossible to hide. I'm a firm believer in that old maxim that 'the wider the man, the wiser the man'." He leant forward as if to share a confidence. "They say Julius Caesar preferred the company of 'wider men'."

"Did he?"

"Brutus was a lean fellow, and we all know what happened to him." He gave me a meaningful look. "Do you understand me, Holmes?"

"Yes, sir, I believe I do."

"Good. Then let's start as we meant to continue. I want a report on the Balance of Payments and how it will affect the funding of the Navy. And this business about flogging in the army – there's a doctor fellow making a song and dance about it. Find out what you can about him. He might be onto something there.

"Then there's this talk of a possible engagement between Prince Wilhelm of Prussia to Augusta Victoria of Schleswig-Holstein[6]. I want your opinion on the implications on the match. And while you're at it, look into the latest reports on the adulteration of food. I had a cup of tea yesterday that tasted of lead pencils. Well, that's all for now.

"Oh, yes, before you go, Holmes, I meant to say you may consider yourself on probation until I've decided whether you're as clever as everyone tells me you are. It'll mean a lower wage of

[6] The engagement was formally announced on 2nd June 1880.

100

course, but you can consider that an incentive to proving your worth. Off you go then, chop, chop."

I left with mixed feelings. I was glad to have retained my position, but a reduction in my salary would make maintaining two households difficult. Economies are going to have to be made and, dare I say, Sherlock might actually have to give some thought to supporting himself.

Accordingly, I called a financial crisis meeting that very same evening at the club and put the situation to him. He seemed disinterested, which came as no great surprise to me, for such is his usual demeanour when discussing anything as inconsequential as how to obtain the means to live, eat and keep a roof over one's head. But when I had to explain the most elementary point to him several times, I came to see his apathy not as insolence but the product of some deeper ill.

"Sherlock, my dear boy, whatever is the matter?" I finally felt moved to ask him.

"Nothing, Mycroft," he had replied absently. "Do go on."

This did not satisfy me, but knowing my brother as I did, if he chose not to tell me the cause of his discomfort, then neither whips nor scorpions would succeed in dragging it out of him. I proceeded with my current line of enquiry, all the while closely observing his

"Put simply I cannot afford to pay your rent at Montague Street."

"I am only short ten shillings this month."

"Ten shillings I do not have to spare."

"Then I shall move into the basement," he declared. "The room has recently become available after the previous tenant died."

"The basement, Sherlock? I should not like to think of any brother of mine dwelling below street level. And this other fellow, the previous tenant, what was the cause of his death? Nothing to do with his surroundings, I trust?"

"Well, now you ask," said he, that sly look of mischief coming to his eyes, "I did hear that the coroner ascribed his death to dry rot. Or was it rising damp? Certainly he looked rather green the last time I saw him."

I disapprove of such flippancy, especially in these circumstances. "You may save what passes as your sense of humour for someone better able to appreciate it," I upbraided him. "May I remind you, Sherlock, that the burden of your rent may soon be beyond my purse. Have you given any thought to the subject of your professional fees?"

"Yes," said he, as though the subject was of the greatest distaste to him. "They are at my discretion, of course. I may on occasion remit them altogether if the case is of sufficient interest."

This, at least, signified some progress in my brother's lackadaisical approach to his finances. "How much have you earned since I saw you last?"

"Net or gross?"

"Either."

"Nothing."

I almost choked on my sherry. "Nothing? Nothing at all?"

"Nothing whatsoever. I have not had a case for over a month."

"Then what have you been doing with yourself?"

"I have been at St Bart's. I have been conducting a few experiments of my own."

"For profit, I trust?"

He sighed theatrically. "Mycroft, have you ever considered that your thoughts turn to money with greater frequency than is altogether decent for a man of your position? Not everything in this world has to have a financial worth. What value can a man assign to knowledge? In the course of my career, it may mean a man's life or it may never be referenced. If I were able to look into the future, I would be at my leisure to pick and choose those areas of interest that would be of use to me, but for now I must by necessity assimilate all and any that may have a bearing on my understanding of crime."

This lengthy discursion seemed to bring him but momentary satisfaction, for I fancied I noticed him wincing and shifting about uncomfortably in his seat. This, coupled with our hall porter's lurid tales of late about the demise of the young and healthy to all manner of mysterious complaints, brought the worst fears to my mind.

"Are you in pain?" I asked with concern. "It's not your feet, is it?"

"You appear to have an obsession with that subject," said he ungraciously. "But you are correct to some extent, although you are in the wrong area. I have toothache, if you must know. I bit down on a hazelnut and cracked my left canine." He fingered his cheek gingerly. "I fear infection has set in."

"Good heavens, Sherlock, is that all? Have you been to the dentist?"

"No."

"Why ever not?"

"Are you aware," said he, "how many people die in the dentist's chair? I could name you at least five cases of murder where the miscreant was judged to have been in professional error and so evaded justice. I can think of no better place to commit murder. The patient is at your mercy. You may do with him what you please. You may cause him pain in the name of repairing his teeth or you may force him to breathe unpleasant vapours in order to spare his sufferings. You may draw a tooth on the pretext of an imminent abscess or you may tell him that all is well and leave him in agonies. No, I have little faith in those who practice the art of dentistry."

It occurred to me whilst listening to this rambling homily

103

that my brother 'doth protest too much'.

"If you are nervous about visiting the dentist, Sherlock, I can recommend a decent fellow you can trust. It is all quite painless, I can assure you. He does it with electricity, you know."

He grimaced. "A sound idea, but all the same, I would rather not."

"Then what will you do? Let your teeth rot in your mouth for the want of a little courage?"

"Courage has nothing to do with it," said he indignantly. "May I remind you that dental work is invariably costly? On the one hand, you urge me to practice parsimony, and on the other, you encourage flagrant expense. You are most capricious this evening, Mycroft."

"If you imagine I would deny you in a question of your health, then you misjudge me. However," I added, alert to the fact that there was more to this than Sherlock was willing to admit, whatever his fine talk of financial considerations, which had never bothered him in the past, "I believe there is another solution to your problem. You don't remember Great-Aunt Euphemia, do you?"

A most eccentric woman, which in our family is nothing out of the ordinary except that Euphemia was a little more eccentric than most, she often boasted that she had never consulted a physician in her life. She had a cure for everything, mostly taken from a penny-book of seventeenth-century herbal remedies that she had bought from a rag-and-bone man at the railway station at Crewe. Indeed, there appeared to be nothing wrong with her until the day she surprised everyone by dying on her 104th birthday after downing a celebratory tankard of ale. The undertaker was of the opinion that she was the healthiest-looking corpse that he had ever seen, and as such took some persuading that she was in fact dead. Even then, he insisted on putting a bell in her coffin so that she could attract attention if she did revive.

I mentioned Euphemia because in some cases her cures did prove effective. In others perhaps less so, such as the time when she 'purchased' a wart from our dear father. This involved casting the coin used in the 'transaction' into the drain where it was to be left, for only then would the wart's removal be assured. To our father, this was an absurd waste of money and he retrieved the coin as soon as Euphemia was gone. For years after, he was heard to say that he was glad he had, for he had put that same coin on a horse that came in at odds of ten to one and made him a pretty profit. The wart, on the other hand, remained where it was, firmly attached to the side of his nose. No doubt Euphemia would have said that this was due to my father's lack of faith.

What I had in mind, however, did not necessitate anything as complicated as the casting of coins into drains, but simply a length of thin twine and a door. A waiter was sent for the required length of twine and this having been duly acquired I affixed one end to the door handle and kept a firm grasp on the other.

"This end," I explained to my brother, "we tie around your tooth. Then we close the door and the twine pulls out your tooth."

So demonstrating, I pushed the door shut with some force. The twine tightened and snapped. I tried again, and this time the door handle came away from the door. Sherlock looked decided unimpressed by my efforts on his behalf and rose to his feet.

"If it's all the same to you, Mycroft," said he, "I would prefer to shift for myself in this matter. This demonstration of yours has not been without interest and some amusement, but I fear we should run out of doors before I run out of teeth. Do not think me ungrateful, but I believe something a little less *outré* is in order."

"You mean to visit a dentist then?"

"Of sorts," said he enigmatically. "I shall keep you informed as to developments."

With that, he left. Some hours later, I received a telegram

105

to the effect that he had had an encounter in the waiting room at Charing Cross station with a ruffian by the name of Matthews, who had obliged him by knocking out the offending tooth. Unconventional it may have been, but I daresay Euphemia would have approved.

Wednesday, 18th August, 1880

August is a most untidy month at the Diogenes.

In common with the other clubs, we are obliged to close our doors to members at least once a year for necessary maintenance caused by 'wear and tear'. Torn blinds, torn curtains, whisky on the carpets, wine on the rugs, broken plates, missing cutlery, holes in the sheets, holes in the tablecloths, burns in the carpets, stains on the walls: it beggars belief that a group as sedentary as the club's members could be responsible for so much damage in so short a time. The plumbing in particular is the bane of the committee's life; what it has cost us in plumbers this year, I dread to think.

How we have managed to stay afloat with such expense is nothing short of a miracle. The annual subscription shall have to be raised next year; we cannot continue to keep the members in snuff, newspapers and toothpicks on the miserly sum of eight guineas a year. Maintenance alone costs us in excess of £1,000 per annum, to say nothing of twice that sum in wages for the club servants.

That being the case, I have been giving due consideration to the methods by which economies may be made. As it happens, this has coincided with the closure of the Diogenes for a period of no less than two weeks. I have been assured by the workmen that it will be no longer; I would be naïve, however, to believe that they were telling me the truth. I have yet to find a builder or tradesman who could deliver within the appointed time, and those who say they can invariably go out of business.

To spare our members the inconvenience of being hungry and homeless, the Diogenes has a reciprocal arrangement with several other clubs for the use of their facilities. The advantage is all on our side. Few can tolerate the monastical silence of the Diogenes, so that we rarely have to accommodate members from other clubs. There was an exception several years ago. A gentleman came to us from the Devoran Club and never left. I would see him about the place occasionally, and never thought much of it.

In many respects, he was the ideal member. He always paid his bills, never hogged the fire and always returned the newspapers to the Reading Room. Our hall porter came to know him by sight and would wave him through without question. No one ever thought to challenge him because he was so well suited to his surroundings. As conversations are not permitted outside of the Strangers' Room and as he was never in there, no one ever spoke a word to him. Had they done so, the imposter might have been discovered sooner.

The revelation came on the day that he was found slumped in his chair, quite dead. It was only then that the club secretary realised that we had had a cuckoo in the nest for six years and he had never once paid his subscription. Since then, we have been wary of men claiming to be from other clubs. We tolerate them, but we make sure that they do not make themselves too comfortable.

As to the present, I have been forced to find solace in the Asparagus Club, several doors along. Founded nineteen years ago on the principle of advancement for *Asparagus officinalis* in an environment where the committed horticulturist can share his ideals with other like-minded gentlemen, it has since been forced to open its doors to the wider vegetable-growing community after membership dropped to five following a scandal involving a turnip.

I have heard people say that the Diogenes is an odd place, but I should say that the Asparagus is something by way of competition. The library contains nothing but tomes on plant husbandry and there lurks in every corner men who know the intimate details of potatoes. Asparagus is rarely on the menu, as the members have never reached a decision over the best method of preparation. They grieve at the thought of asparagus soup, and to ask for it is to bring down curses upon one's head.

Despite this, it suited my purposes for the time being. This being the height of summer, many of the club's members had returned to their estates to see that their prize marrows and pumpkins were being adequately watered. As such, I had the Asparagus Club largely to myself, save for those members from the Diogenes who had followed me. I tended to look favourably upon them for their choice; less so, those fellows who had taken up residence at the Athenaeum or the Carlton Club. It seems to me to suggest a tendency towards sociability that does not accord with the Diogenes Club's founding principles.

I had thought the Asparagus would afford me some privacy, but in that my expectations have been thwarted. At half-past six, an impertinent fellow dragged his chair over to mine and had the gall to address me directly.

"Mr Mycroft Holmes?" he asked.

I looked at him over my paper, in a manner which I hope suggested my displeasure at the interruption. A stringy man of middle years with grizzled features and a military air, the care and anxiety I read in his furrowed brows and bloodshot eyes informed me that more was troubling him than the paucity of the club's reading material.

"I answer to that name, sir. And you are?"

"Major Julius Prendergast." He hesitated. "I understand you have a brother."

"You understand correctly."

"I hear he's a rather clever fellow when it comes to solving *problems*."

I must confess to being troubled when people use unnecessary inflections. Rather than prevaricate, they would be better advised to state their business plainly. This vain attempt at delicacy only serves to irritate.

"You have been accused of cheating at cards," I stated.

Prendergast's mouth fell open. "You know," he gasped. "Then it is already too late."

"Calm yourself, Major. I have heard nothing."

This seemed to reassure him, although it was not the guarantee of confidentiality for which he hoped. As a general rule, I do not concern myself with petty gossip. Our hall porter is a font of information in that regard, but getting it from him requires asking after his health, and after a long discussion about the state of his chest, which, according to him, has been deteriorating for years, one loses one's appetite for the affairs of other men.

"Then how the deuce did you know?" asked Prendergast.

"That you have taken shelter here at the Asparagus speaks of some estrangement from your usual club. Had it been for a transgression of the rules, you would have been forewarned. Nor would you be asking for my brother's assistance had you been caught tipping the waiters or removing food from the dining room. There are only two instances where one's club would consider immediate expulsion without prior warning: failure to repay a debt of honour and a charge of cheating at cards. If the first, you would have gone to your bank manager. The latter, therefore, seemed the more likely of the two."

Prendergast nodded furiously. "You are correct, Mr Holmes. I have been accused unjustly. The club has threatened expulsion if the charge stands. If I cannot prove my innocence to their satisfaction, then I must take my case before the courts."

"That is the usual course of action. To which club do you allude?"

"The Tankerville. Do you know it?"

Naturally I was familiar with the establishment. It had acquired a reputation as being one of those places that forever court controversy. Only last year, a member was excluded for smuggling his wife into the club. It says a good deal about her powers of acting – or indeed a want of observation on the part of the staff and members – that the deception was only discovered over dinner one evening when her moustache fell into the Windsor soup. Even then, the waiter was most tactful, merely scooping the offending appendage from the bowl and presenting it to her in the ladle. The problem came when she stuck it back on upside down and she was labelled a bounder for cultivating such an outrageous style on her upper lip.

Given their other problems, I could see why the club's committee was keen to have this matter resolved.

"Do you have reason to believe you would lose a civil case for slander?" I asked.

The Major looked desperate. "There are three witnesses to my alleged crime."

"And yet you insist you are innocent."

111

"That I am, sir. If I am expelled from my clubs, I shall never be able to show my face in London again. I could survive expulsion from the Tankerville, but not from the Asparagus. I have many enemies in the carrot-growing world who would rejoice at my disgrace."

"Quite so. Grievous indeed, Major Prendergast."

I spoke from personal knowledge. Uncle Hadrian had suffered the indignity of expulsion from his club after he had been warned repeatedly about putting his feet on the table of the Smoking Room. It was not his boots they minded so much as the spurs he insisted on wearing at all times of the day and night, much to the consternation of his wife. Considering that he had never ridden a horse in his life, it was fair to say they were superfluous to his needs. When the club servants threatened mutiny because of the time they spent removing marks from the furniture, the committee took the view that they needed the staff more than they needed Uncle Hadrian.

He was a broken man after that. He took to sitting in trees in public parks imitating bird calls to avoid going home, until the day he convinced himself he could fly and tried to follow a flock of starlings into the air with fatal consequences. Had he chosen a smaller tree, I believe he would still be with us today rather than ending up halfway to Fulham on the upper deck of the Kilburn and Kensington omnibus.

Because of this, I did have some sympathy with Prendergast's plight. Loath as I am to encourage my brother in his profitless hobby, it did occur to me that I could not chastise his lack of funds on the one hand and refuse to send a client his way when the opportunity arises on the other. Accordingly, I despatched the boy with a message, and a little over twenty minutes later, the steward came to inform me that the hall porter had detained a gentleman who was asking for me.

"He claims to be your brother, Mr Holmes," said the stoic fellow.

"How does he look?" I asked.

"Hungry," came his reply.

"Then it is undoubtedly my brother. I shall see him in the Strangers' Room."

By the time I arrived, without Prendergast, to prepare my sibling for the novel experience of receiving a potential client, Sherlock had already made himself comfortable and was glancing through *The Pea-Growers' Chronicle*.

"I received your missive," said he, somewhat insolently when I addressed him. "As it happens, Mycroft, I was coming to see you today in any case."

"How did you know where I would be?"

"An intimate knowledge of your habits. Of the clubs which are available to you, this was the most likely. I had considered the Archivists' Club, but thought you might consider it too lively."

"Quite so. When I was last there, they were in mourning because one of their books had gone missing. Very noisy they were about it, too. You wouldn't think the loss of a copy of the 1877 *Dibble's Somerset Almanac* would warrant weeping and the gnashing of teeth. Now, brother, what was your errand?"

He did me the courtesy of not bothering to pretend that this was anything other than a call upon either my time or my purse.

"I am in need of a favour."

"The last time you said that," I interjected, "you gave me that wretched dog of yours. If you mean to leave him with me again, I must disappoint you."

"Toby is back with Mr Sherman," said he, somewhat archly.

"Then it is money. Come, sir, do not beat about the bush."

113

"Very well. There is the small matter of a fine."

"What is it this time?"

"A trifling business concerning a public nuisance."

This came as no surprise to me. I have long said that my sibling was a nuisance, and to have it recognised publicly felt like vindication.

"I have been charged with exercising horses to the annoyance of certain persons, namely a local magistrate."

I was certain I was likely to be disappointed by the answer, but I had to ask.

"It was for a case," he replied. "Several performers at the Hoxton Hippodrome were trampled to death when Tarleton, the Equine Wonder, galloped from the stage in the course of an act that it had performed in excess of two hundred and fifty times. I was attempting to ascertain if a horse could be trained to gallop over a body on command. If so, then the creature was used as a means of murdering five people."

"And what were your findings?"

Sherlock shook his head. "I was arrested before the experiment reached a satisfactory conclusion. The beast I hired broke free and escaped. I eventually found him in a nearby garden, eating the nasturtiums. The owner of the property was not swayed by my explanation." He had the gall to maintain his composure as he spoke without displaying a shred of contrition. "I would be obliged if you would intervene, Mycroft. I have better things to do with my time than spend several nights in the cells."

"As it happens, Sherlock, I may be in a position to help you," I announced. "There is a gentleman here at the club in need of your services. Take his case, pocket his fee – and then you can pay the fine yourself."

With no other option, he had no choice but to accept. Not that he was taking the case under duress, for I observed a spark of interest. Indeed, I have not seen him so animated since the age of eleven when Aunt Elvira was accused of attempting to poison the ladies of the Cursewell Mothers' Union with her shortbread biscuits. Her motive was said to be their undue criticism of her apple pudding, although, having tasted it myself, I could find little to praise. She was exonerated, however, when it was discovered that the butter she had purchased had been rancid. As Aunt Elvira had lost her sense of smell when her pet tortoise had fallen on her head when she had been trying to extricate it from the ivy of a ten-foot wall, the police were not inclined to take the matter any further. Despite that, it created a good deal of ill feeling, and the vicar was never again able to look upon melted ice-cream without having attacks of biliousness.

Prendergast was pathetically grateful for our interest, and we listened as he poured out his woes.

"It was yesterday evening," he explained. "I was playing cards at the club with Rear-Admiral Palgrave, Lord Valentine and Henry Englewick. I was winning too; luck seemed to be on my side. Well, I stepped outside for a moment, and when I returned, I knew something was wrong. No sooner had we resumed the game than Englewick accused me of dealing from the bottom of the pack. It was lies, of course, but the other two men supported him."

He wrung his hands in abject misery. "What am I to do? Unless I act now, the rumours shall be the ruin of me. Word has already reached the ear of my fiancée. She said she will break off our engagement by Friday if I am not exonerated."

"A woman of little sentiment," I remarked.

"On the contrary," said Prendergast, "Rosamund is a most sensitive soul. I would not see her touched by a breath of scandal. I would rather die."

"I doubt it will come to that, Major," said my brother. "Tell me, where was Englewick sitting?"

"To my right."

"And you are right-handed."

The Major stared at him. "However did you know that?"

"A cursory examination of your hands reveals that the middle finger of your right hand bears a callous to protect the joint against the pressure of the pen," I explained.

Sherlock gave me a fleeting look of annoyance, as might be expected when one resents the stealing of one's thunder. "Where were the others seated?"

"The Rear-Admiral to my left, and Valentine opposite me."

"How much money had you taken from Englewick?"

"Fifty. He had taken twice that much from me the previous evening."

"The others?"

"Palgrave about the same. Valentine a little more. He was new to the club."

"How long have you known Englewick?"

"Three years or more. He is a regular at the card tables."

"Rear-Admiral Palgrave," I interjected. "If memory serves, he lost his right eye and three fingers of his right hand to a tiger in India."

"Yes, that is correct," Prendergast confirmed. "He wore a patch until recently, but now he has a glass eye."

"Does he? Now that is interesting."

That seemed to me to settle the question. Sherlock asked several irrelevant questions until, finally satisfied, he assured our grieving companion that he would have the matter resolved within the hour.

"Heaven bless you, Mr Holmes," said Prendergast, grasping his hand with all the fervour of a man rescued from stormy seas. "But will you not tell me the meaning of this accused business?"

"I should prefer to wait until I have all the facts to hand."

116

"Thank you, sir. If there is anything I can do, you have only to ask. If I thought you would not be offended, I would offer you money–"

"My brother has too many debts to be offended," I said, much to Sherlock's displeasure.

"Then when you tell me who is responsible, I shall see that you are compensated for your time," said Prendergast. "Good evening to you both."

"Must you interfere?" said Sherlock when Prendergast had gone.

"I begin to see why you enjoy these petty problems, brother," I replied. "They are an amusing way to pass the evening. You have reached some conclusion in the case?"

"Indeed."

"Then would you care for a wager?" I wrote the name of the person responsible for the slander, along with the motive, on a half sheet of the club's stationery. I folded it and held it aloft. "If I am wrong, I shall pay your fine. If I am right, you shall give me five guineas. Your client is in the mood to be generous."

Entirely as I expected, the wager was accepted. Sherlock can never resist the opportunity to prove me wrong; that he has yet to do so never deters him.

He took the paper and read the name. A smile spread across his features and his eyes gleamed in what I took to be triumph.

"My dear Mycroft, your reasoning is faulty," said he, preening like a peacock. "I believe I am ahead of you this time. Valentine is the obvious culprit. He was a newcomer to the tables, and resented the Major's good fortune at the expense of his own. His word would not carry as much weight as the other men, so he sowed the seeds of the apple of discord when the Major left the table. Thus incensed, Englewick saw what he expected to see. I shall examine him upon this point, of course."

117

"I have no complaint with your argument as to why Englewick was primed to deliver the accusation," I retorted. "I doubt he could swear to having seen Prendergast dealing from the bottom in court. Being right-handed and with Englewick seated to his right, Prendergast's hand would have concealed the pack of cards he was holding from Englewick's view."

"I will allow that Valentine's word, as a new member, would have carried less weight than that of the Rear-Admiral. But we can rule him out because his injuries would have made his right side, where Prendergast was seated, difficult to see. He would have held the cards in his left hand, and naturally turned slightly in that direction to compensate for the loss of his vision. Which makes your belief that he was responsible for the accusation baffling, Mycroft."

I sat back in my chair and regarded Sherlock gravely. "Do you remember Cousin Emmeline? She had her heart set upon the local greengrocer in her youth. She bought a new hat one day and trimmed it with cherries in the hope of attracting his attention. Regrettably, she attracted only Lord Topsfield's flock of pigeons, but that is not the moral of the story. Emmeline would brook no competition; I seem to recall one unfortunate incident where she had a fight with the vicar's daughter when she caught her ordering an extra pound of apples. Affairs of the heart may make a person act in the most extraordinary ways."

Sherlock appeared none the wiser, and so I was compelled to continue.

"The preference of the glass eye over the patch is revealing. It made me suspect that the Rear-Admiral had some romantic expectation. Coupled with the fiancée's sudden desire to be released from the engagement, I am led to believe that the pair have formed an attachment and concocted this plan between them. If you examine the fair Rosamund, Sherlock, I fear you may find her wanting in affection for the Major."

118

He would not have it, nor did I expect his immediate capitulation. Before eight o'clock, however, the boy had brought in a letter for me. The enveloped contained a promissory note from my brother for the sum of five guineas.

I have a mind to have it framed and hung upon the wall of my office, for I doubt I shall ever see the money. My brother can have the fame, but I shall have the satisfaction of having won our little game. A victory is still a victory, after all, even if things do not go entirely to plan, as Cousin Emmeline said when she married Lord Topsfield.

Saturday, 11ᵗʰ September, 1880

Whosoever said that the road to hell was paved with good intentions must have kept a diary, for only those who had tried the experiment knows how easy it is to let the habit slide. I find myself faced with a plethora of empty pages since my last entry and not a wit of how to fill them. I fancy that I have *lived* those days and must have done something, but for the life of me, I cannot think what.

This suggests to me either that I have been very busy and had not the time to write, or that I was underemployed and had nothing worthwhile to record. Certainly, if this week is anything to go by, then the latter would seem to be the answer to my problem. Considering that I find myself under a new administration that has made certain promises to the electorate who, having duly elected their representatives on this platform, now not unreasonably expect those promises to be kept, I would have expected more diligence and signs of activity.

Instead, the Cabinet has talked of cricket and very little else. From what I have gleaned – having no interest in the game myself – something called a 'Test Match' between England and Australia has been held at the Oval this week, significant for reasons which seem to elude me[7]. I was wont to frown on such frivolity in the working week, but I was reminded of that old adage about all work and no play making the Prime Minister a dull boy. Furthermore, I was told in no uncertain terms that I was still on my 'maiden over' and if I did not want to be 'out for a duck', I should keep my opinions to myself, lest I find myself on 'a sticky wicket'.

Cricketing terminology aside, I believe I have, as the Prime Minister wished, proved my worth on more occasions than I already care to recall. My salary, however, remains unchanged. How Sherlock is surviving, I cannot say, suffice to presume that he seems to be managing – or at least conveying a good impression of a fellow who is.

We do not talk of money when he comes to the club to dine, but of club-footed Italians and their abominable wives, elderly Russian women and strange rituals conducted in country houses leading to the discovery of dead butlers and battered old jewels. It is a strange existence my brother leads, but it seems to give him great satisfaction, whatever I may think of it.

Sherlock may have been on my mind this morning, but it was another of our scattered and objectionable family who commandeered my attention, namely the scatter-brained and very objectionable Cousin Aubrey.

If later generations come to these journals of mine seeking enlightenment as to the ways and mores of the nineteenth-century,

---

[7] The first cricket Test Match to be played in England took place between England and Australia on the 6th to the 8th September 1880.

I fear the name of Aubrey Tacitus Holmes may loom large. I hope I have not been too unkind to the fellow; he is family, after all. If I have been ungenerous, however, it is only because it is difficult to find anything to say in his favour. His reputation hangs over our respective heads like a decayed hammerbeam roof: impressive to behold, but ready to bring disaster tumbling down upon us at any moment.

It is not entirely his fault. The blame must lie to some extent with that great Roman orator, Cicero, for it was a line in one of his books, *De Natura Decorum*, that gave Aubrey notions above his station and intelligence: *"No great man ever existed who did not enjoy some portion of divine inspiration."*

Poor Aubrey has been in search of divine inspiration ever since. If he ever finds it, he may have it in him to make his name famous; for the time being, however, he is simply infamous as being one of the oddest men in London.

This should not blind one to his faults, however, and to fall into Aubrey's clutches is a fate I should not wish upon any of my enemies. Avoidance of the fellow is the safest course of action, and I should have kept to this resolve had events not overtaken me. It was an unhappy series of circumstances and I cannot help but taste the bitter gall of displeasure and embarrassment whenever I recall them. By committing them to paper, I hope to dispel their power over me. Failing that, I shall take one of my powders and trust that I do not have nightmares.

It so happened that I had had to deviate from my usual Saturday routine to visit Piccadilly and the tobacconist who supplies my order of snuff. The last packet I had received had the unmistakeable odour of damp about it, and I was incensed enough not to trust to the boy to remedy the situation, but to take my grievances personally to Mr Happenny.

He was effusive with his apologies, blaming his oversight on the Employers' Liability Act which had come into force last

Tuesday[8]. Since news of it had reached his ears, so Mr Happenny told me, he had not enjoyed a peaceful night's sleep for worry that Mrs Elliot might fall from her high stool beside the cash register and do herself an injury. If she did, so he claimed, paying her compensation would lead to his ruin. Thus, in this state of anxiety, he had accidently mixed up his old stock with his new and had no end of complaints since.

The answer to his problem, as I advised him, was elementary: provide Mrs Elliot with a more suitable chair or bring the till down to her level.

This seemed to please him immensely, and with many expressions of gratitude, he thanked me for my patience and hoped that he could rely upon my custom in the future.

I left the shop in a contented frame of mind. That was my first mistake. When circumstances seem to be moving in one's favour, that is usually the time calamity strikes. In my case, it was my decision to make my way home by way of St James's Square. It seemed safe enough, but unbeknown to me, disaster was waiting for me around the corner.

So it was that on entering York Street, Cousin Aubrey suddenly appeared.

"Cousin Mycroft," he oozed. "You look prosperous."

By prosperous, I gathered that he was making some oblique reference to my girth. This, coming from a man who has chosen to curl his hair and grow a moustache, knowing that a host of our shared ancestors have always abhorred such ostentation, was somewhat hard to take, and had I not been caught off my guard, I should have told him so. As it was, I was desperately seeking a means of escape and finding none.

"Really, Mycroft," he went on, "it is most fortuitous your being here."

---

[8] The first Employers' Liability Act providing compensation for workers for injuries that were not their own fault came into force on 7th September 1880.

Members of our family only employ the word 'fortuitous' when it applies to their own situation. I sensed an appeal for money was imminent.

"Why, for my exhibition of course," he elaborated. "Didn't you get my invitation? I had them engraved, you know. It cost me a pretty penny, I can tell you."

"Invitation?" I said vaguely.

"I sent them out to all the family. It appears I chose a most inauspicious date. Everyone said they were busy today."

When I thought about it, I recalled that I had received something that bore Aubrey's handwriting. I had filed it in the wastepaper basket unread, a rare error on my part which was about to cost me dear.

"However," said he with evident pleasure, "you are here, and that makes all the difference."

"It does?"

"One cannot have a grand opening if one has no one to attend it."

"Forgive me, Aubrey, a grand opening of what?"

Pride beamed from every inch of his features. "My paintings. I'm an artist now."

This did not come as too much of a surprise to me. Aubrey has tried most things in his long and varied career. That he would turn his hand to artistic endeavours was inevitable.

"And what is it that you paint?" I asked.

"Portraits," he stated. "You should come and sit for me, Mycroft. Rarely have I seen such a subject worthy of capturing in oils."

I was still undecided whether this was meant to be a compliment or otherwise when Aubrey let out a sudden exclamation of delight.

"Cousin Sherlock!" cried he. "Well met, my dear fellow, well met. How are you?"

That my luckless brother had fallen into Aubrey's trap unwittingly was evident from his appalled expression. He had rounded the corner unawares as I had and Aubrey had pounced, grasping his hand and shaking it with such force that it made his teeth rattle.

"Aubrey," said Sherlock tightly. "A pleasure, as always. Mycroft, what are you doing here?"

"I could ask you the same question."

"I have a complaint to make about my latest order of tobacco."

"Was it damp?"

"Decidedly."

"Mr Happenny has problems of his own."

"It seems to be the common lot," said he, with a wary glance at our beaming cousin, whose broad smile resembled that of a cat who finds two mice at his mercy. "The last we heard of you, Aubrey, you were protesting against the march of progress."

"With little success, Sherlock," he replied, shaking his head. "I am a lone voice crying in the wilderness. By the time people realise that I am right, it will be too late. The fate of mankind is sealed, I fear. A hundred years from now, walking will be anathema to the human race. We will have lost the use of our legs in preference to conveyance by the accursed metal monsters of the railways."

"A hundred years from now, I shall be past caring," said I. "Well, Aubrey, good to have met you again, but really I must be on my way."

"Won't you stay for the opening?" said he, in a voice that ached with disappointment.

"An opening?" asked my brother. "Of what?"

"I am an artist," declared Aubrey. "I have a selection of my finest works on exhibition in the gallery across the road. Come, Cousins, and I shall show you the fruits of my labours."

Had we not been brought up to allow manners to take precedence over good common sense, we should have taken the opportunity when Aubrey turned his back to make a run for it. We did not, however. Sherlock and I shouldered our burden and followed him into the gallery.

It was not as bad as I had feared. Knowing Aubrey as I did, I expected something outrageous and provocative. Instead, around the walls were a number of innocuous and unrecognisable faces, the sort of work that might embarrass a child of five, but nothing to unduly upset the sensibilities of society.

What puzzled me was the gallery owner's profound nervousness when he saw that Aubrey had managed to attract an audience. The man was sweating and shaking and appeared to be on the verge of collapse. This I took to be at first nothing more than the usual effect Aubrey had on people, although the thought did cross my mind that there was more to this exhibition than a few ill-painted faces.

These suspicions were confirmed when Aubrey directed us to a large canvas covered by a sheet on an easel set in the centre of the gallery.

"Cousins, I want you to be the first to see my masterpiece," he declared. "Mycroft, Sherlock, I give you *'Nocturne in Yellow and Puce'*."

With a flourish, he pulled away the sheet and I saw at once the reason for the gallery owner's concern. On a bed of dishevelled linen, a buxom nude of Rubenesque proportions reclined and stared out at us, her ample charms evident for all to see and little concealed by the flaming red hair that fell about her shoulders.

I do not consider myself to be one of those men who shock easily. I was, however, taken aback by this product of Aubrey's fevered imagination. Moreover, there are some sights not suitable for young impressionable minds and my first thought was to clap my hand over Sherlock's eyes to preserve his fragile innocence.

"What are you doing, Mycroft?" said he, pushing my hand away. "I've already seen what it is."

"Magnificent, isn't she?" said Aubrey approvingly. "Her name is Bessie MacDonald. She's my muse. She inspired me!"

"That much is evident."

I gave my brother a look of reproof for such an indelicate remark. "Aubrey, it's a nude," I said.

He sniffed with self-importance. "If you don't mind, Mycroft, I prefer to call it a celebration of the female form. And no one has form finer than Bessie MacDonald."

"Call it what you like, I absolutely forbid you to put this work on public show."

"Come now, Mycroft," said Sherlock. "It is not too bad. The brushwork leaves a little to be desired but if you take a few paces back it improves on its appearance."

"I am not talking about its artistic merit. I am referring to the subject matter. Aubrey, if not for your own reputation, consider the rest of the family."

"Why? They never consider me. Ah, more visitors."

As Aubrey darted away, I made haste to return the cover to this alarming portrayal of Bessie MacDonald. Sherlock was no help and found the whole episode somewhat amusing. I was in the process of straightening the sheet when my day suddenly took a turn for the worse.

"Good heavens, Mycroft Holmes, I thought I recognised you."

"Good heavens, Prime Minister," said I. "Good day, sir. What brings you to Piccadilly?"

"Problem with my cigars." He was peering intently over my shoulder. "What's that you've got there?"

"Nothing in particular, Prime Minister."

127

"You won't mind my having a look then."

He was a good deal more agile than I would have given him credit for a man of his age. Before I could interject, he had whipped the sheet away from the canvas and Bessie MacDonald was revealed once more in all her yellow and puce finery. An awkward silence descended. I had nothing to say, and the Prime Minister I was sure was lost for words. At that same moment, Aubrey took it upon himself to put in an appearance.

"You like it?" he enquired hopefully.

"Like it?" boomed the Prime Minister. "I think it's the best thing I've seen in a long time. Are you the artist?"

"Why, yes, I am."

"She's a fine-looking lass and no mistake."

Aubrey beamed again. "I tried to capture her very essence."

"You certainly did that." He narrowed his eyes as he stared at our cousin. "I know you, don't I? Aubrey Holmes, isn't it? Yes, I thought so. Saw you on stage a while back. *Hamlet*, I think it was."

"An experience that has bad memories for me, sir. The other actors were philistines. They had no appreciation for my art." Aubrey grimaced as if to banish the memory and then assumed a level of unctuousness that was embarrassing to watch. "In terms of appreciation, I hope you don't think I'm taking a liberty in asking sixty guineas for the painting."

"Worth every penny, I daresay, but I can't take it, Mr Holmes. The wife wouldn't understand. She likes pictures of animals. What about you, young man?" said he turning to Sherlock. "What do you like?"

"I'm rather partial to the *Newgate Calendar*."

"Are you now?" said the Prime Minister, not in the least perplexed by this somewhat irrelevant reply. "And who would you be?"

"This is my younger brother, Mr Sherlock Holmes. Sherlock, this is Sir Piers Renfrew."

"Ah, the enquiry agent."

"Consulting detective," said Sherlock, shaking the Prime Minister's offered hand.

"Well, young man, I've heard good things about you from this brother of yours. Would you be willing to put those brains of yours to use for your government?"

"For a fee?"

"Sherlock," I said reprovingly. One would wish to make a good impression, and souring a commission from the highest quarters with the suggestion of money seemed to me to be somewhat uncouth.

"No, he's quite right," said Sir Piers. "The labourer is worthy of his hire. How do you expect him to live, Mycroft, if you insist on giving his services away for nothing? No wonder the poor fellow is half-starved if you keep selling him short. I'll see you're suitably rewarded, Mr Holmes. Now, if you'll come with me, I'll explain what the problem is."

The irony was of course that I had been advocating a more business-like approach to his affairs for some time. Now I stood accused of under-appreciating my brother's worth. Tales of this incident would be doing the rounds of Whitehall for some time to come and I would be the poorer for it.

With that in mind, I left the gallery in ill-humour and retreated to the sanity of my club. The ending of the day did not improve upon its beginning, for a telegram arrived as I was leaving for home from Aubrey, informing me that he had sold his painting for eighty guineas and that several gentlemen had expressed a hope that the London art scene would be seeing a good deal more of Bessie MacDonald in the future.

It only goes to prove that divine inspiration is to be found in the most unlikely of places.

Wednesday, 1ˢᵗ December, 1880

Heaven forgive me for committing such thoughts as these to paper, but today an event has occurred which I thought would never come to pass.

Put simply, my brother has come to live with me. I cannot help feeling that no good will come of it.

It is entirely my own fault. Were I harder of heart, I should have turned him out on the street and saved myself a good deal of time and inconvenience.

Instead, I relented and took pity on him, with one stroke both satisfying my conscience and damning myself to a petty hell thereafter.

But I am getting ahead of myself. One must start at the beginning of this sorry little drama, which for me began at a quarter to five when, after a trying day at Whitehall, I sought sanctuary in my club to find that Sherlock had arrived there before me.

I had my first inkling that all was not well when the Honourable Lucas Bainbridge, a man so red in the face that his nose has a positive glow about it, accosted me in the hall and informed me that he intended to report my diabolical treatment of the club's facilities to the committee. Since I am on that very same committee, I suggested that he might as well tell me the nature of my transgression.

"This is not a boarding house for your hapless relatives," said he. "That you allow them to treat it so makes you, in my mind, a bounder, sir!"

Naturally I denied the charge most vigorously.

"It's that brother of yours! He has been here the best part of the afternoon and seems intent on staying. It's a liberty, Mr Holmes, a confounded liberty."

On that point, I had to agree. Sherlock was not a member, but as my brother, by extension, had honorary member status or, failing that, was considered to be my guest. This meant it was my responsibility to see that he behaved himself; equally, he was obliged to behave himself and not embarrass me.

However, it has always been my contention that my brother's *raison d'être* seems to be just that, that he was put upon this earth with the sole intention of making my existence as trying as possible. I do not say he does it out of malice, except that it happens, whether by accident or design.

Abusing the club's facilities – Bainbridge was not specific as to what this had involved – would certainly raise questions at the next committee meeting, and, as he had no official status, the penalty would no doubt fall on me. If he continued in this vein, I could well find myself excluded from my own club.

With this in mind, I apologised for my brother's behaviour and said I would ensure that whatever he had done would not happen again. This mollified Bainbridge to some extent and he went away muttering something about there being other clubs in London for fellows who had a social bent and that fraternising had no place in the Diogenes.

A worrying image came to mind that Sherlock had done the unthinkable and had invaded the club with a number of his carousing friends. This thought I dismissed with equal alacrity. For one, I have never known Sherlock to carouse, and two, to my knowledge he has no friends of a carousing nature. Come to that, I am not altogether sure whether he has any friends at all, which, depending on one's particular point of view, may either be a good or a bad thing. A friend in need is a confounded nuisance, our dear father always used to say, and when one is in need oneself, one's only friend may be the bank manager.

In this instance, Sherlock's friendlessness was to prove unfortunate for me, because as usual it was to his elder sibling he turned in his hour of need. I found him in the Strangers' Room, surrounded by his worldly possessions, namely two bags and a trunk, blithely explaining to the steward how he had arrived at his theory of how the man's younger sister had recently married by a close observation of his shoes.

The steward was impressed. I was less so, for not only was it patently obvious that several items of his attire had been bought new for the occasion and, since he was unmarried himself, this could only point to the nuptials of a member of his family – and who more so than a cherished sister, for one does not make so much effort for reviled brothers, a fact to which I can readily testify – but because Sherlock was keeping the man from his duties.

We at the Diogenes are not in the habit of entertaining the staff. Needless to say, tipping is absolutely forbidden. We pay a good wage and expect good service in return. I now understood the reason for Bainbridge's indignation; clearly he had been kept waiting for his usual afternoon libation while the staff were otherwise engaged with my brother.

"Sherlock, what are you doing here?" I wanted to know when we were alone.

"I should have thought that obvious," said he.

"You have been expelled from your lodgings."

"That is putting it mildly, Mycroft. Thrown onto the street might be more accurate."

"Because you have failed to pay the rent." I adopted my best disapproving demeanour. "I trust you have not come to me for money, for I have little enough to cover my own expenses. What happened to the fee you received from the Prime Minister?"

"You mean for solving that trifling affair involving the under-gardener, the cook, and the missing wheelbarrow? Not quite what I would call working for one's government, although the case did have some features about it that made it worthy of my interest."

"You are prevaricating, brother."

"It was a handsome sum, I cannot deny. I thought I should purchase something in memory of a most intriguing business."

"I would have never taken you for a sentimentalist, Sherlock."

"Ordinarily no, but in this case, it was too good a chance to miss. Would you believe, a genuine Stradivarius for only fifty-five shillings?"

I took my usual seat. This interview promised to be a long one.

"In matter of fact, I do not believe it. How do you know it is genuine? I understand there are any number of fakes and forgeries on the market."

"You would have to see it to understand. It has the 'feel' of age about it."

133

"The same could be said for a good many people. It does not necessarily follow that one would naturally want to give them a home. However," I said, pressing on while my brother was at a disadvantage, "it does not answer the question what you intend to do now you are homeless."

He took a long time to reply. Bitter experience has taught me to be wary of these episodes, since they usually bode ill for someone, more often than not myself.

"I was rather hoping that you might consider—"

"Certainly not."

"You might let me finish, Mycroft," said he indignantly.

"You do not need to do so, for I know full well what you were about to say. Correct me if I am wrong, but you were about to ask whether I could put you up for a few days. The answer is a most emphatic no."

"I see." There was something about his tone that gave me pause. "You would turn your own brother away in his hour of need."

"Yes," I replied, "if his name was Sherlock. Any other brother would be perfectly welcome to stay."

"We do not have any other brothers."

"Then I shall not expect them to come calling. I am sorry, my dear boy, but my decision is final."

"Ah," said he, rubbing his chin thoughtfully. Again I was on my guard, not that one should ever relax in Sherlock's presence, but, as in the vicinity of a viper, be ever prepared for the unexpected stroke. "Well, in that case," he went on unconcernedly, "I shall have to throw myself on the mercy of Cousin Aubrey. I'm sure he could put me up in his studio. That is, if the delectable Bessie MacDonald doesn't object."

I have, on occasion, been rather too critical of my brother. At times, I wonder if he is not a changeling, dropped upon our doorstep and adopted by our guileless parents believing him a gift

134

from some kindly benefactor. Physically, we have little in common, he having a rather Mephistophelean visage – which is why I have always discouraged him from growing a beard; one should try to overcome one's shortcomings, not embrace them – and rather too much energy, a characteristic which if anyone knows our family is not shared by any of our close relations.

Indeed, our Great-Grandfather Hieronymus took care never to move further than five yards from his favourite armchair from the age of sixty-six until his demise in his ninety-eighth year. My sympathy was with his physician; pressed for the cause of death, he could only attribute it to stagnation. I do not say he was far wrong. Certainly there was always the odour of ponds about Great-Grandfather Hieronymus.

Back to my brother, however, for all our differences in appearance, from time to time he is able to rise to the occasion to prove that we do share more than a taste for expensive tobacco. Bringing Cousin Aubrey in the argument was just the sort of underhand tactic that generations of our family have for centuries worked long and hard to perfect.

I had to admire his cunning; certainly I should not have had the gall to play that particular card were the tables turned. However, any pride I was feeling for this rare accomplishment on his part of having backed me into a corner was tempered by an equal feeling of annoyance that I had been outmanoeuvred. He knew I would never agree to his staying with Cousin Aubrey. The alternative, his staying with me, was unthinkable but in the circumstances, it was the lesser of the two evils.

Grudgingly, I agreed.

It was perhaps the worst decision of my adult life.

Now several hours later, I find that my home is not my own. Never have I seen so much paraphernalia disgorged from a single trunk. No sooner had I persuaded my landlady that the arrangement was a temporary one, and I had given my assurance that he would behave in a manner commensurate with his station than he had proceeded to make himself comfortable by making my two small rooms as untidy as his own.

As a rule, I prefer to maintain order on the basis that it keeps the cleaning to a minimum – and my landlady happy – and because one may always know where to lay one's hand on any particular item without having to turn out every drawer and cupboard to find it. Sherlock, conversely, believes that a tidy room, like a tidy shop, indicates inactivity.

Mess, to his mind, is equated with industry; thus, the messier the room, the busier the person.

So it is, that I find my floor littered with old newspapers, a heap of musty books beneath my bed, false eyebrows stuck to my shaving mirror – at least I hope that is what they are – and something vaguely chemical boiling away in a chamber pot. If this is a taste of what is to come, I fear one of us may not make it alive to Christmas.

Friday, 24ᵗʰ December, 1880

Whosoever invented Christmas has a good deal for which to answer.

I do not lay the blame for this at the door of our Creator, but rather with those who believe there is something good to be said for close familial contact at a time when the shops are shut and the servants will insist on taking a holiday. There is no escaping Christmas; he who would close his door on the outside world and yell 'humbug' from his upper storeys is branded a 'Scrooge' and worse things besides.

Which is hard on me, for this year 'humbug' is a word that has been very much on my lips these past few days. On more than one occasion, I have caught myself sneering at Christmas trees. Sellers of penny carols have been dismissed with refusals curt enough to turn their cheery smiles upside down. Indeed, it was all

I could do to muster the energy to purchase something suitable for my godchild. I am clearly not in the Christmas spirit.

That I am less so than in previous years, I blame not on rising middle-age, but on the pernicious presence of my resident hobgoblin, a nasty, messy little beast by the name of Sherlock, who has the gall to call himself my brother.

I have always prided myself on being a tolerant man, but three and one half weeks of occupying the same space have near pushed me to the breaking point. Many a time have I contemplated fratricide when I have seen my floor strewn with ash and paper, or thrust my toe in my slipper to find a plug of tobacco has beaten me to it. On such occasions, I have clenched my fists and ground my teeth, and reminded myself that man hath but a short time to live and is full of misery, a statement which would seem to have been made with long-suffering elder siblings in mind.

It is not that I mind untidiness; sometimes one must create disorder to achieve order. What I cannot understand is the refusal never to tidy up after oneself. Sherlock tells me he has a system. He tells me that he can lay his hand upon any item at any time.

However, I have witnessed him tear my rooms apart in search of an insignificant newspaper report about some such crime or another. I have seen newsprint fall and flurry like so much grimy snow about him, to be then trodden under foot when some such fit takes him off in pursuit of another line of enquiry. I have had to console my poor landlady when the sight of my chambers has reduced her to tears, and this with kind words and money for the employ of a boy to shovel the waste to the sides of the room to create a pathway for us to walk.

Clearly this situation cannot be allowed to continue. I fear for my sanity and my brother's continued well-being, for I am increasingly convinced that not a jury in the land would convict me for having buckled under such provocation. A gentleman of certain years needs his rooms to himself and whatever sympathy he may feel for a younger brother's plight should not sway him from that consideration. Some may call it selfish; I call it self-preservation. Sherlock will have to go.

Turning him out on Christmas Eve, however, has the feel of some ghastly music hall melodrama about it. I had borne it thus far and a few more days would not hurt. During the day, our points of contact were few. Sherlock busied himself doing something or another and I had the refuge of my club.

At least I *thought* I had the refuge of my club. When I arrived this evening, it was to be informed that someone had been asking after me. A chill ran through me when I considered the possibility that it might be an acquaintance wanting to wish me a 'Happy Christmas'. I was able to suppress that thought with the knowledge that I eschewed acquaintances for that very reason. Had it been my brother, the hall porter would have said so – and I would have been able to detect that objectionable whiff of the laboratory that seems to be his chosen cologne at the moment.

"It was a crying man, Mr Holmes," explained the noble fellow when I pressed him for details. "Never seen a fellow in such a state. We had to bring him in because people kept falling over him where he was on the doorstep."

"Does this fellow have a name?" I enquired.

"Yes, he did tell me," said the porter, scratching his head. "Queer sort of name it was too. Like a girl. Ah, I remember. Audrey he said his name was."

I had that sudden feeling of dread one gets before enquiring about the balance of one's banking account after a heavy month of expenditure.

"Do you mean *Aubrey*?"

"That's the name, sir. We put him in the Strangers' Room. He stopped crying when we gave him a brandy." A low moan of anguish rent the hallowed silence of the club. "I think he's started again now though."

I followed the howls and found Aubrey sprawled on the hearth rug in a state of inebriation and self-pity. When he saw me, he crawled across the floor and clung like a drowning man to the hem of my coat.

"She's abandoned me, Mycroft," he wailed.

"Who has abandoned you?" I said, trying to extract myself from his clutches.

"My muse. My goddess. My flower of delight. My queen of paradise—"

"I take it you are referring to Miss MacDonald?" I interjected.

"Bessie," he sighed, somewhere between remembered passion and present misery. "Sweet Bessie. Dear Bessie. Buxom Bessie—"

"Aubrey, please," I upbraided him. "Remember where you are. The members come here to get away from that sort of thing." I manoeuvred him into a chair and removed his half-filled glass from his immediate vicinity. "So, she has left you, has she? I cannot say I'm surprised. You were always a fool where women were concerned. I seem to remember something about a lady in Grimsby."

"Mrs Fortinbrass," said he with fond remembrance. "What a woman!"

"She threatened to sue you for breach of promise."

"A misunderstanding. I never said I would marry her."

"She had your letters, Aubrey."

"Forged," he declared. "I would never commit a thing like that to paper."

"And the engagement ring?"

"The woman was delusional. She bought it herself."

"It had your initials on it."

140

"Pah, they could have been anyone's!"

"The jeweller remembered you buying it."

"I don't see how. His glasses were as thick as bottle tops. I'd wager he didn't see a thing."

"How do you know he wore glasses if you had never met the man?"

Aubrey considered, saw that he was in a hole and decided to stop digging. "I admit I made a mistake with Mrs Fortinbrass, but Bessie – dear, darling Bessie! – she was different. To her I gave my heart!"

"Indeed. Where is she now?"

"Gone off with a rich banker from Peckham." His face crumpled. "What can he give her that I could not?"

"I would have thought that was self-evident."

"Money isn't everything," he wailed. "I offered her immortality."

"Only on canvas," I reminded him.

"Isn't that enough?"

I was about to remark that Aubrey was making a fine stab at answering his own questions. He was, however, too wrapped up in his own misery to have appreciated my comment and I left him to continue in a similar vein.

"I cannot paint without her," he rambled on. "My life is over."

I glanced at my watch. Time was pressing and Aubrey was becoming tedious.

"I shall throw myself into the Thames this very night," he declared, rising to his feet with an overly-dramatic wringing of his hands, "and bid goodbye to this cruel world. Then Bessie shall know how she has broken my poor heart!"

"The gesture would be a wasted one, Aubrey," I said. "Miss MacDonald doesn't strike me as the sentimental type. If anything, your death might be seen as a boon. I understand the work of a deceased artist is valued more highly than that of his living counterpart."

"Then I shall live and confound them all! I shall run away to sea and make my fortune in some far-flung land. And then, *then* Bessie will see how wrong she was to spurn the honest love I offered her!"

"Is that wise?" I ventured. "I seem to remember an incident where you suffered an attack of *mal de mer* on the Serpentine and had to be rescued by an elderly lady."

This perplexed him but for a moment. "Then I shall join the Foreign Legion! Yes, that's the life for a Romantic like me."

"Do you speak French?"

"I can order coffee in five languages, Mycroft," said he indignantly.

"That should be useful in the desert."

I would have said more, but at that moment Aubrey believed he had found himself an unlikely ally in the shape of Sherlock, who had arrived, late as usual, at my invitation for our traditional Christmas Eve repast at my club.

"Cousin Sherlock," Aubrey declared, "Mycroft says I'm not fit to join the Foreign Legion."

"I daresay he's correct," replied my brother. "I understand they are particular as to whom they take."

"Then I am just their man! I shall leave without delay!" He clasped my hand and near dislocated my shoulder. "Thank you, Mycroft. I am a changed man thanks to you."

"Good heavens," Sherlock remarked, "what did you do to him?"

"Not I," I replied. "It was Bessie MacDonald."

"Ah, yes, I heard. She left him for a wealthier man."

From where my brother gets his information never ceases to be a source of fascination to me. "And how, pray, do you know that?"

"*Everybody* knows, Mycroft," said he in that tone of voice that suggested I was woefully behind the times. "You should get out more. You spend far too much time buried in Whitehall."

"When the day comes that I find myself taking advice from you, brother, I shall retire. You are late, by the way."

"I had... a slight delay."

His pause troubled me, as did the faint aroma of sulphur that hung about his clothes. That, allied to the black smudges I could see on his ears and what looked like ash on his shoes began to alert me to the fact that all was not well.

"Sherlock, has something happened?"

"No," he said lightly enough.

"Sherlock," I growled.

I am not accustomed to 'growling', but on occasion I find it works wonders with my brother in eliciting the honest truth.

"Well, there was an *incident*."

"Go on."

"A small matter of an unfortunate chemical reaction. The authorities over-reacted, as they always do."

"In what way 'over-reacted'?"

"It was mostly smoke, you understand. There really was no need to evacuate the building."

I felt the hairs rising on the back of my neck. "Which building?"

He hesitated a long time. "Where you have your rooms." He must have seen the expression on my face for he hastily continued. "It was much ado about nothing, if you ask me. A new coat of paint on the ceiling and no one would be any the wiser. As for arresting your landlady—"

"They arrested Mrs Cresswell?"

"For a public nuisance offence. She was soon released. As for the summons—"

I had heard enough. "Sherlock, this time you have gone too far. I have been patient with you, and you have abused my hospitality. I have no alternative but to ask you to find other accommodation."

"We shall have to do so in any case," said he languidly. "The building inspector said the house would not be habitable for several days until the fumes have cleared."

"There is no 'we' about it, sir. You will leave this very night."

"Mycroft, now you are over-reacting. It was only a small explosion."

"The size is immaterial. Perhaps you do not understand me, brother. I am giving you notice with immediate effect."

He stared at me in that insolent way of his. "You're turning me out, on Christmas Eve, your own brother?"

"Indeed. Sooner, if possible."

"Very well, since you insist, I shall leave. Do you realise, Mycroft, that I shall have to find myself somewhere else to spend the night." His gaze travelled upwards. "The rooms upstairs…?"

"Are for the exclusive use of members of this club. You are not a member. You are here under sufferance, and I believe I have suffered enough at your hands. Out with you!"

"Well, I must say this is very uncharitable, denying me room at the inn, so to speak. And how very apt at this time of year."

"Since we are quoting chapter and verse, perhaps you would do well to remember that I am not my brother's keeper. A spell in the gutter might do you the world of good."

"I might catch my death of cold."

"I am not that fortunate."

On that note, we parted, acrimoniously. In the hours that followed, I have had cause to regret my words. Not knowing where my brother is – and on a cold night such as this – is infinitely worse than having him underfoot. I had been angry, as any fellow had a right to be after hearing that his rooms had been ruined and his landlady arrested, and I had said rash things. I had not meant them, of course. One says things in the heat of an argument that would be better left unsaid.

That he has gone missing is a judgement upon me. My punishment is now that I must spend this night worrying about his whereabouts. I have no doubt that he has made himself comfortable somewhere; the lurking suspicion remains, however, that he is wandering the streets and seeking out a doorway in which to sleep.

Worse, the thought occurs that he has joined forces with Cousin Aubrey to spite me and even now is making his way to join the Foreign Legion.

Well, I daresay I shall find out on the morrow. Until then, an uncomfortable night awaits me in the club's bedrooms. I regret now suggesting to the committee that we purchase hard mattresses to discourage the members from abusing this privilege.

It is ever the case that one learns the error of one's ways too late.

Saturday, 1ˢᵗ January, 1881

I recall exactly one year ago making the extravagant claim that I would religiously keep a diary to record those events of my daily life, significant or otherwise. With the birth of a new year – a blank page in the history of the world, if the literary analogy is continued – I find myself questioning whether my enterprise has been a success. Looking back over a year's worth of nonsense about christenings, cleaning ladies and elections, I find a good deal about Sherlock and very little about anything else.

What this tells me is that my brother takes up more of my time than is advisable. Either that or my days are singularly uninteresting compared to the misadventures of my family and younger sibling. One does not mind such an imbalance, but one could wish for rather less in the way of the sort of turgid melodrama in which my kin excels.

My hopes for the next twelve months, therefore, are for a quieter life. I do not suppose for one moment that I shall get it, but I live in hopes, none the less.

I am likely to be disappointed if the last week is anything by which to judge. Following my contretemps with Sherlock, I had neither seen hide nor hair of him since Christmas Eve. This has come to me as something of a disagreeable surprise. I had expected him to turn up bold and unrepentant for Christmas lunch, but he did not. I had expected some word from him, but received none. What began as indignation on my part gradually became anxiety of the gravest order.

Indeed, the matter had become so serious that I was obliged to register my concerns at the local police station. They expressed some sympathy and sent me on my way with meaningless reassurances that 'he would turn up sooner or later'. Dead or alive seemed to me an appropriate rejoinder, to which they suggested I enquire at the local mortuary to see if he was numbered amongst the unclaimed bodies. This I duly did and came away happily frustrated, since neither of the bodies of the two elderly ladies offered for my inspection matched his physical description at all.

My mind was not settled, however. I am used to Sherlock disappearing for weeks on end and have long since ceased to be offended by his lack of communication. But when the lure of the chef's finest offering – a bird within a bird within a bird, a *tour de force* of his culinary skill, involving a goose, a duck, and a partridge – fails to draw him from his lair, I begin to fancy that all is not well with him. We have taken our Christmas lunch together for more years than I care to remember; that he chose to set aside tradition I fear bodes ill.

Finally, after an exhausting week scanning newspaper columns for reports of the unclaimed dead and asking young constables who appear to me barely old enough to be out of short trousers whether they had seen my brother, finally – and I do repeat myself to express the heady mixture of relief and annoyance that accompanied this momentous occurrence – *finally* did Sherlock deign to put in an appearance.

He wandered into the club apparently without a care in the world, ordered himself a whisky, and proceeded to hog the fire in the Smoking Room. As witness to this cavalier display of arrogance, I harboured hopes that his coat tails would catch fire and teach him a lesson.

"Where have you been this last week?" I asked.

"Working," said he in that irritatingly laconic manner of his.

"Over Christmas?"

"This may come as a surprise to you, Mycroft, but some people are obliged to work whatever the season. While you take your ease, the rest of us have to manage as best we can."

This remark I chose to ignore, having no relevance to the conversation in hand. "Working, you say? Am I to deduce from this pronouncement, brother, that you have come to your senses at last and found some decent form of employment that does not involve you mixing with unsavoury elements or wearing make-up?"

"Actor's greasepaint, Mycroft."

"Our dear mother used to wear rouge, Sherlock."

"So did our father."

"He imagined himself a passable actor."

"That is where we differ. My disguises are an essential element of my trade."

I groaned. "You still insist upon calling it by that lamentable name."

"Only because it annoys you," he grinned. "Very well, my profession then."

"You do not deny that you pursue it still?"

"Indeed I do, and with hopes that this year will prove more fruitful than last."

A waft of smoke rose from his general direction. I was about to reach for the jug of water to put him out when I noticed he had helped himself to one of the club's cigars. I was able to relax again, though feeling somewhat nettled at the liberty he had taken in emptying the cigar box without a thought for other people.

"I've given what you said the last time we talked a great deal of thought," he went on. "It occurs to me that you may have been somewhat justified, even if your reaction was grossly melodramatic."

"I am glad you see my point of view," I replied, unsure whether I felt more flattered than insulted by his remark.

"As a matter of fact, I was looking at the situation from my standpoint, Mycroft. This shilly-shallying between addresses has done me no favours. My clients never know where to find me from one day to the next. What I need is a permanent address. To that end, I have made enquires and have found suitable premises in Baker Street."

"Ah, yes," said I, settling myself back in my chair in my usual attitude of repose that I adopt when about to impart the benefit of my years of knowledge. Impressing people, particularly one's younger sibling, is one of the few pleasures of possessing stores of out of the way and seemingly useless information. In Sherlock's case, reminding him that he has at least one mental superior serves to keep him in check. "Baker Street, laid out by one William Baker, a speculative builder, in the mid-eighteenth century, as I recall, hence the name, and on land leased from the Portman Estate. Home at one time to William Pitt the Younger and Sarah Siddons. Today it is considered respectable, but not fashionable."

"More importantly, it is affordable."

"Yes, I wondered when the question of money would raise its ugly head. Just how do you intend to pay your rent, Sherlock?"

He did not reply immediately, but took to rearranging the tangled fibres of the hearth rug with the toe of his boot. This procrastination gave me grounds to suspect the worst.

"You haven't done something rash?" I asked with concern.

"That rather depends on your definition of 'rash'."

"Good heavens, you haven't sold yourself to medical science?"

"Mycroft, what ineffable nonsense you talk."

"When I see a man with his hands covered in strips of sticking plaster, I am led to assume that either he has been spending time in the company of rats or that he has met with some terrible accident. It isn't rats, is it? Tell me you haven't been sleeping in one of those appalling boarding houses where men sleep on a washing line."

"No, your lack of charity did not reduce me to that."

If he said it to prick my conscience, he was wasting his time. I was immune from his barbs and gibes, not least because he had obviously been making himself comfortable somewhere without a thought for those left to worry about his absence from the Christmas luncheon table.

"If you must know, I was conducting an experiment," he explained. "It's where I have been this past week, at St Bart's. I needed blood, and mine own was readily at hand."

"Some might say your studies were positively ghoulish, Sherlock."

"Some lack the imagination to see where my investigations might lead. I have discovered a new and infallible test for blood stains, Mycroft!"

I am sorry to say I was suitably unimpressed. Sherlock, however, was all enthusiasm and seemed quite to have forgotten the direction of our conversation.

"Fascinating, I'm sure. However, you were telling me about this 'rash' arrangement you've made for the rent."

"Oh, that," said he indifferently. "I have found someone willing to split the cost with me."

I almost choked on my brandy. "Who? It's not Cousin Aubrey, is it?"

"Certainly not." His tone suggested that I should have known better than to ask. "It was strangely fortuitous. I happened to mention to Stamford that I was looking for someone to share the burden of the Baker Street tenancy, and a couple of hours later he produces this fellow who was also looking for rooms. We are going tomorrow to look over the place to see if it meets with our approval."

"You're sharing with a stranger who walked in off the street?"

"He is not a stranger. His name is Dr John Watson. An ex-army medical man, discharged with a wound pension and down on his luck. He has a bull-pup and he smokes ships. What else does one need to know?"

There are times when my brother, for all his intelligence, displays a propensity for recklessness that would make any other man weep.

"What's wrong with him?" I asked sternly.

"He took a bullet in the shoulder."

"No, I mean what's *wrong* with him?"

He gave me a blank look.

"Speaking as someone who has tried the experiment, I do not understand why any man in full possession of his faculties would willingly share rooms with you, Sherlock. How do you know this Watson fellow isn't a wandering lunatic?" An alternative and less excusable explanation suggested itself to me. "My dear boy, you were honest with him?"

151

"To a point," said he, arranging himself insouciantly in the opposite armchair. "I told him I play the violin, I conduct experiments, and occasionally I get down in the dumps."

"What about the *other* things?"

"What *other* things?"

"Would you care for a list?"

He rose and threw the remains of his cigar into the fire. "I knew this was a mistake," said he ungraciously. "You never change, Mycroft. Always quick to censure and slow to praise."

"Having spent the better part of last week evicted from my apartment due to your irresponsible behaviour, I am entitled to speak as I find. The truth, brother, which you find so unpalatable, is that you are impossible to live with!"

"I may be difficult, but a few noxious fumes are nothing compared to the strain of sharing rooms with you, Mycroft. You snore."

"I do not."

"And you talk in your sleep."

"I refute that accusation absolutely."

"Moreover, you are a petty tyrant who extends the hand of charity only to snatch it away when the arrangement becomes inconvenient. I deserve a medal for having endured in silence at your hands for so long."

I was appalled and angered by his ingratitude.

"Then go, live in Baker Street," I declared. "I wash my hands of you. If this Watson fellow turns out to be a deranged murderer and slaughters you in your bed, do not come running to me!"

An acrimonious parting is not the best way in which to begin a new year. Sherlock did his level best to make as much noise in his departure as was humanly possible, thus incurring the wrath of the other club members. For my part, I was hurt by his accusations. I have never snored in my life. To think that I was concerned for his welfare; had I been wiser and less benevolent, I should have not wasted a single moment worrying about the ungrateful little whelp.

I half hope the arrangement with this Dr Watson does fall through. It would give me great pleasure to tell him that I told him so.

Friday, 1st April, 1881

Again, I turn to my diary to find that I have been less than conscientious in maintaining regular entries. Three long months and many blank pages separate this from my last entry. I seem to recall noting that I wished for rather less of my brother and more of my own affairs. I have had the one, but not the other. Sherlock has been noticeable by his absence these past three months, and I appear to have led a singularly uninteresting life, unworthy of recording even in its meanest detail.

However, life is not all drama – how tiresome it would be if that were so. Our lives are filled with trivial little happenings, which do not necessarily require our committing to paper. Many are forgotten as soon as they are over. If the minutiae are infinitely important, as I have often told Sherlock, then that does not make them worthy of memorialising. It does not profit me to know that I had my shoes cleaned on Thursday or the chimneys swept on Monday. I pride myself on the considerable store of information on obscure subject matter that I carry about in my head, but even I must make exceptions.

Therefore, I have been content to lead a trivial existence and equally content to forget it. That I take up my pen now means that an event has occurred worthy of my recalling in my dotage. And as always it concerns my ubiquitous brother, Sherlock.

Even without him, my day has been an eventful one. I understand from our office boy that today is known in some quarters as the day of the 'April Fool', hence the sugar instead of salt in the Whitehall dining room and usual advertisements for the annual washing of the lions at the Zoological Gardens.

Such excesses, I am glad to report, have never reached the ears of the Prime Minister, a man who does not suffer fools lightly. The axe has not been slow to fall in some quarters, and I have long been aware that I was still on probation. How long that condition was likely to remain was a subject I have been unwilling to press, given the man's uncertain temperament. Catch him on a bad day and one might well find oneself unemployed before lunch.

Treading on eggshells is the recommended approach. That and doing the tasks allotted to me to the best of my ability in the hope that merit will persuade him to reinstate my full wage.

I had been diligently following this course of action when, at our morning meeting, the Prime Minister intimated that matters had been resolved to his satisfaction and he was growing tired of my presence. I was about to leave, aware all the while that the Prime Minister's critical gaze had never wavered from my person, when suddenly he spoke.

"I noticed an account of your Sherlock in the *Echo* a while back, Holmes," said he. "Making quite a name for himself, by all accounts."

155

One grows used to the eccentricities of the Prime Minister's speech. All the same, hearing my brother termed as 'my Sherlock' brought to mind the image of an undisciplined pup.

"I'm surprised you didn't mention it," he pressed.

The truth of the matter was that this was the first I had heard of it. The Diogenes does not take the *Echo*, on the grounds that radical newspapers tend to be noisy and inspire rowdiness in their readers. To say as much to the Prime Minister would be tantamount to immediate dismissal; thus, I chose to be diplomatic.

"I would not presume upon your interest, sir."

"Not presume, sir?" said he, a flush coming to his cheeks. "Whitehall is no place for shrinking violets, Holmes."

"No, sir."

"However, I admire your restraint. This position of mine attracts no end of sycophants and boot-lickers, all after advancement for themselves and their families. Even the gardener is up to it! The confounded fellow asked me if I knew of anyone who needed their hedges trimmed. I admire enterprise, but there's a limit."

"Indeed, Prime Minister."

"Your brother is different, however," said he, wagging a bony finger in my direction. "Reading between the lines it seems to me that he ran rings around Scotland Yard in that last case of his. The boy has talent."

"Yes, he does, sir."

"I'm glad you agree. That's what I like about you, Holmes. You know what loyalty to one's family means. All too often brothers are at loggerheads. If they aren't cutting one another off, they're running off with each other's sweethearts."

The note of bitterness in his voice made me wonder if he spoke from personal experience.

"But not you, eh?" he continued. "You support that brother of yours. I like that. I admire it even. Do you know, when

I came to office, I thought you were another of those Whitehall fatheads with a sinecure to pay your way and very little going on up here." He tapped the side of his head. "Granted, you know your stuff, Holmes, but it's your relationship with that brother of yours that changed my mind. So I've come to a decision. I'm putting you back on a full wage."

"Thank you, Prime Minister."

He waved this consideration aside. "Don't be too hasty, sir. You won't thank me when you hear the problem I want your opinion on next week. Now, out with you, and convey my regards to that brother of yours."

My conscience gave me trouble for the rest of the afternoon, so much so that I was compelled to send a telegram to Sherlock inviting him to join me at the Diogenes that evening. On arriving at my club, it was to be informed that Mr Holmes was waiting for me in the Strangers' Room. It was not, as I had hoped, my brother, but our lamentable cousin, Aubrey.

"I thought you were bound for the Foreign Legion," I questioned him over whisky and soda.

"So I was, Cousin, so I was. I didn't mind the desert so much, but do you know they had the audacity to expect me to fight? Me, behind a bayonet – I ask you! And so unreasonable! I said it would never do, and they said they didn't want me." He wrinkled his nose. "Well, their loss, I say."

"What have you been doing with yourself since then?"

"I lingered a while in Paris. It *inspired* me, Cousin, oh, I cannot tell you how much! It brought out my finer instincts. It fired my imagination. The high life, the low life, and everything in-between. I have been reborn, Mycroft! I am the phoenix newly risen!"

As he was making this florid declaration, springing to his feet and gesticulating wildly, the door opened and Sherlock entered. We are used to Aubrey's ways, so it was not surprise that

157

registered upon his face, but rather dismay at seeing the fellow returned from his aborted adventures.

"Cousin Sherlock, just in time," Aubrey enthused. "I was just explaining to Mycroft about my latest venture. How are you, by the way? Well, I trust? Good. In that case, sit yourself down. Gentleman, I have decided that I am to be... a *poet!*"

We said nothing. It was inevitable that Aubrey should try his hand at poetry sooner or later. I could only hope that it did not take the same form as his art.

"Would you care to hear a sample of my work?" said he. "Of course, I must be careful. I have been warned against plagiarists. We are alone?"

Alone, apart from old Hetherington Wadley-Matthews, who had fallen into a slumber several hours ago, his usual occupation at this time in the afternoon, which for a man of ninety-four was his right. As his visitors had long since gone, having been unable to wake him, we left him to his nap.

"Proceed, Aubrey," I said.

He assumed an affected stance, tilted his chin and fixed his gaze on some far distant point. "I have entitled this piece, '*Ode to Bessie*'." He cleared his throat with a degree of self-importance. "*Shall I compare Bessie to a summer's day?*"

I glanced at Sherlock. His expression mirrored my own.

"*She is more lovely and more temperate. Rough winds do shake the darling buds of—*"

"Forgive me, Aubrey, it's been done before," I interjected.

"Has it?" He seemed greatly affronted. "Confound the fellow! I daresay he took his inspiration from me."

"I shouldn't think so," said Sherlock. "He has been dead for nigh on two hundred and fifty years. You may have heard of him. Shakespeare?"

"I thought it sounded familiar," said Aubrey. "No matter, it wasn't one of my best pieces. Here, I have another. I call it, '*I am a man*'."

"It is always advisable to select a subject with which one is intimately acquainted," I observed.

"Very well then, here goes." Again, Aubrey coughed and his face assumed such an expression of concentration that I began to believe he was unwell. "*I am a man. I have made my own plan. I shall cast off my clothes and eat tarte tatin.*" He paused. "That's as far as I've got. What do you think?"

"What is the significance of the 'tarte tatin'?" asked Sherlock in all seriousness.

"It rhymed with 'man' and 'plan'. Does it matter?"

"Undoubtedly it matters. If one is to be great artist, one cannot simply throw words together haphazardly. When you are questioned, Aubrey, do not say that you chose the words lightly. You should imply that it has some symbolic meaning, accessible only to those who are intelligent enough to understand it. That way, everyone will declare you are a genius for fear of admitting that they have not the slightest clue what you are talking about and appearing diminished in the eyes of their peers."

Aubrey beamed. "My dear Cousin, I raise my glass to you. You are a genius."

"Yes, I know. And if you're looking for word to rhyme with your current scheme, may I suggest 'ban'."

"*I am a man,*" Aubrey mused. "*I have a plan. I shall cast off my clothes and eat tarte tatin. I shall defy the ban!*" He clapped with evident delight. "Extraordinary! I don't suppose you have a word to rhyme with 'orange', do you? Never mind. I am on my way. By this time next year, I shall be Poet Laureate. Cousins, I depart. Destiny awaits!"

"Was that wise?" I questioned my brother after Aubrey had galloped from our presence.

159

"You would prefer I tell him the truth?"

"Certainly not. I do question the wisdom of encouraging him, however."

"With Aubrey, I have observed that the more encouragement he gets, the faster his enthusiasm wanes. I give it a month. He will make a fool of himself, declare the world of literature to be farcical and find some other interest."

"Very diplomatic of you, brother."

"It is a skill one develops with rapidity when one is sharing lodgings."

"Ah, yes, how is your fellow tenant?"

"He has not murdered me in my bed yet." He smiled. "In fairness, I must say it has proved to be a satisfactory arrangement. I own that I am not the easiest devil with which to share common space—"

I made a noise of agreement. Sherlock cast an annoyed glance in my direction.

"But I have endeavoured to live a less turbulent existence in the past few months. You would not recognise me, Mycroft. I am quiet in my ways and regular of habit. I go to bed early and rise with the lark. This has made me a subject of interest. The old expression about still waters running deep has something to recommend it."

I asked him quite what he meant.

"He has attempted to make a study of me, this fellow Watson," said he with amusement. "Whilst I believed him to be slumbering in his chair, he was compiling lists of my limits and achievements. He believes me to have a profound knowledge of chemistry, to be well-up on sensational literature, ignorant of philosophy and astronomy and hopeless in the field of practical gardening." He laughed. "A fair assessment, wouldn't you say?"

"He sounds like a hopeless busybody to me."

"No, no. He simply displays that innate curiosity inherent to the nature of the man of intellect. What else is a convalescing invalid to do but to study his surroundings and fellow man as a relief from tedium?"

There was something about his tone that alerted me that the interest was not entirely one-sided. "You speak, Sherlock, as though you have done something to relieve this poor devil's burden."

"As a matter of fact, I have. I invited him to join me on a case[9]. Don't look so shocked, Mycroft. He expressed an interest in my work – and some doubts. What was more natural than that I gave him a practical demonstration? The case was an intriguing one – a classic case of revenge across two continents – and I fancy the good doctor was impressed, so much so that he intends to write his own account of the business, to correct the inaccuracies of the newspaper reports. My merits should be publicly recognised, so he tells me. Indeed, he got very heated about it and started quoting Latin at me!"

Sherlock has all the natural modesty of a Cheshire cat. To say that he appeared as pleased as Punch at this prospect would be a gross understatement. For my part, I felt a few words of brotherly caution would not go amiss.

"Fame is an uncertain animal, brother. It is true to say that those who have it wish it not, whilst those without it crave it all the more. It was Pope who spoke succinctly of the man '*damned to everlasting fame*'. There is wisdom in those words."

"He also spoke of those who '*damn with faint praise*'," said he icily. "But I do take your point. From what little I know of Watson, I have my doubts as to what form this account will take.

---

[9]Readers of the accounts of the cases of Sherlock Holmes will know that there is considerable debate over the dating of '*A Study in Scarlet*'. Unfortunately, Mycroft Holmes's diary entries shed no light on the problem.

161

On the other hand, I am not sure that I am not a little flattered by the attention. There is something in having one's own amanuensis, after all."

When my brother preens excessively, I begin to worry. "When am I to meet this paragon?" I enquired.

"Meet him?" Sherlock sat up abruptly. "Heavens, no. I daresay he already considers me a little out of the ordinary. I would not wish to confirm his suspicions by subjecting him to the horrors of the family. I shudder to think what he would make of Aubrey. Besides, what interest could you possibly have in meeting him?"

"From the way you have been talking, my dear boy, it seems plainly obvious to me that you have acquired what might be described as 'a friend'."

As a general rule, our dear father always maintained an aversion to the forming of friendships. The best of friends, so he said, was ready money, or failing that, an old dog. People came rather lower down his list. I am afraid it is an inheritance that we have received in full.

"You deny it?" I asked.

"Utterly." He hesitated. "I would rather call him 'an acquaintance'."

I shook my head. "I have my acquaintances, none of whom have ever done me the honour of wanting to chronicle my doings."

"That is because you have no doings to chronicle, Mycroft, at least not any that could be safely published."

"One day you may be surprised," I declared. "These past few years, I have been in the habit of keeping a journal."

Sherlock brightened. "Am I in it?"

"There are several passing references to the various members of my family."

162

"Indeed. You must let me read it some time. It will amuse me no end to see how my brother fills his days."

"I fancy that privilege shall be mine. When is this account of your case to be published?"

"When it is written," said he obliquely. "Now, if you will excuse me, Mycroft, I told Watson I would meet him for supper at Romano's. You don't mind, do you?"

In matter of fact, I did mind, having invited him with the expectation of dining together on the club's best poached salmon. Since I was too tactful to say so, however, I dined alone, nursed my grievances with a good port and ended my evening wondering if my brother was fully aware of the perilous road he was treading.

Monday, 8ᵗʰ February, 1886

Our dear father was a great believer in the axiom that the devil is in the detail. Sherlock has since taken to peddling the notion as if he had invented it; he has had the gall on more than one occasion to tell me that the 'little things are infinitely the most important'.

What he cannot claim, however, is our father's particular experience in this field, which led him to the original observation. As he always recounted it, he had attended a ball at his own father's command. Our grandfather, it seems, had a view to marrying him off and thus saving the expense of his board and lodging. He had soon tired of the evening, being neither a graceful dancer nor what may be called an interesting conversationalist. He had requested his hat, gloves and cane, and the footman had duly vanished on this mission and never returned. Our father eventually found what he thought were the missing items on a hall table and asked the pretty young woman sitting beside them: "Are these mine?"

What she heard, however, was: "Be mine." To this, she understandably answered "Yes", for she had been ignored for the better part of the evening. On this basis, it was my mother's understanding that a contract of marriage had been made. Since our grandfather could not countenance our father to breaking his word, they were married a month later.

By all accounts, it was a tolerable match, about which neither party ever expressed any strong feeling either way. Our grandfather maintained that it saved him £45.7s.3d. per annum, and in that sense it had been a success. Whatever really happened that night will never be known, except that Father forever warned us about the need for clarity, in speech especially.

This comes to mind now, because of an outbreak of what one might call 'romantic expectations' at Whitehall. Sir Rowland Dour, the Home Secretary, has taken to wearing a rose in his buttonhole. He has been observed loitering in corridors and sighing mournfully whenever a young lady passed by. It is true to say that such behaviour invariably finds its own reward, for there was a regrettable incident only yesterday when he mistook our new cleaning lady, Mrs Swale, for one of the typists. What she did to him for such impertinence, I cannot speculate. Needless to say, he has refrained from loitering ever since.

The source of such tomfoolery, I am reliably informed, is entirely due to the date. Sunday being Valentine's Day, every young woman has hopes of receiving a postcard from a secret admirer with verses about roses being red and violets blue.

I have endeavoured to discourage such behaviour in my office, but it has not stopped an outbreak of mischief. Twice today the typist brought a document to me for inspection, and twice I have had to reprimand her for giggling. I began to suspect that all was not well when Lord Rousingham's Parliamentary Private

Secretary burst out laughing when I gave him my report on the recent unrest in the capital. That it was followed by a hearty, "Well done, old man", seemed to me to be the herald of further strife to come.

The mystery was finally solved by that guardian of our morals, Mrs Swale. A humourless woman of advanced years, who could have put the Puritans to shame, her habit of scowling at all and sundry forbids any conversation other than that which is absolutely necessary. When the Prime Minister once asked her if she was well, she reproached him for wasting the good Lord's air on irrelevancies.

Brevity suits me well enough; when I look back over the trouble we have had with our previous cleaners, I consider Mrs Swale to be a paragon of virtue. Whitehall has become a good deal more sober and sensible since her arrival, and I daresay we are all the better for it.

It came as something of a surprise, therefore, to find myself falling short of her standards. Having brought my tea and one plain biscuit, she was about to leave my office when I saw her eyebrows rise.

"Lasciviousness caused the downfall of Rome, you know," said she sternly.

"Amongst other things," I replied, wondering what had led to such a remark.

"My husband warned me about working here," she went on, folding her arms in that manner beloved by the disgruntled. "He said it was no place for a respectable woman. Really, I thought better of you, Mr Holmes. I expect such behaviour from the clerks, but not a man in your position!"

Given that all I had said to her thus far was, "Thank you, Mrs Swale", I was at a loss to see how I had given offence. She obliged by pointing at the window behind me.

"Don't deny it," she crowed. "It's there for all to see."

Scrawled on the outside of the glass, in the grime left by the smoke of the city, were the words, 'Be My Valentine', written so as to be legible from inside my room.

I could not deny its existence, but I did deny authorship. The fault lay with our window-cleaner. This is not the first time I have had trouble with the man. He imagines himself a lothario; mostly, however, he is a lazy fellow. I have had words with him in the past for not pressing his rag into the corners of the glass. This message I took to be his petty act of revenge.

Having explained myself to Mrs Swale, she was inclined, despite her initial reservations, to overlook the incident in view of my former good behaviour. She promised to clean the glass, but warned me that she would be 'keeping an eye on me' in the future.

The charge is unwarranted, certainly. But as the Bard, said: *"Be thou as chaste as ice, as pure as snow, thou shalt not escape calumny."* Calumny or, as in our father's case, marriage. I can only be grateful that Mrs Swale already has a husband or I should have found myself in the same situation.

Mrs Swale and Valentine's Day aside, the better part of the afternoon was taken up with news of a disturbance, when a crowd of several thousand left a meeting in Trafalgar Square and proceeded along Pall Mall and into Oxford Street. Windows have been broken and property vandalised[10].

As a result, I spent most of the late afternoon in conference with the Prime Minister discussing the situation. After I emerged some hours later, it was to find a message waiting for me, bearing the grievous news that the Diogenes Club had been

---

[10] Following a peaceful mass rally against unemployment in Trafalgar Square, a group of several thousand men set off towards Pall Mall, throwing stones at the windows of clubs in St James's Street, before raiding shops in Piccadilly. On reaching Hyde Park, a smaller group continued along Oxford Street before being dispersed by the police at New Bond Street. Three men were arrested and one constable was injured.

attacked. My immediate attendance was requested. The members were in a state of shock and needed reassurance.

When I arrived, I found several of them waiting for me on the pavement outside, surveying the sad remains of one of the club's potted box hedges. The hall porter had been tending it and its partner for five years or more, so the club secretary told me, and he had had hopes of fashioning it into a peacock. This brought a tear to the eye of Sir Roger Fairbrother, and he, along with several others, removed their hats in due reverence.

Personally, I had never liked the plant and could work up no sorrow for its loss. I had only agreed to its placement by the entrance when I was near to being over-ruled by the committee because a member had had the audacity to complain that our façade was 'rather dull'. That it had met its end seemed less a reason for regret and more cause for celebration.

"You say the rioters did this?" I asked.

"Certainly they did," said Sir Roger. "It was a terrible thing to see, Holmes. We were in fear of our lives. They smashed the windows of the Carlton Club, you know."

Granted, there were papers blowing up the street, along with scattered debris and broken branches. Further up Pall Mall, several policemen were wandering about with notebooks recording the damage done to windows and buildings.

"But not ours," I noted. "Just the one pot. Why not the other?"

"One is enough," said Sir Roger imperiously. "What are you going to do about it, Holmes? This is an outrage."

"I agree. But I cannot lay the blame with the rioters. See here, in the compost, there is a clear print of an outstretched hand. Nor are there any boot prints in the spilled earth, as there are in the mud of the gutter. It seems to me that this was knocked over after the riot. It should be easy enough to identify the culprit. The hand print shows that he does not wear a ring."

Several of the gathered members looked at their hands. My attention, however, was drawn to Sir Walpole Makepeace, who immediately put both hands behind his back.

I have had my suspicions about Sir Walpole from the first. He came to us with three letters of recommendation, which is three too many by my estimation. If a man can call upon three people to testify to his unsociability, it suggests that he is not as curmudgeonly as he would have us believe. On this basis, I was all for rejecting his application. But because another member of the committee knew him and said he was the most foul-tempered, objectionable old devil ever to draw breath, the majority were in favour of his acceptance.

I do wonder, in light of this and other unfavourable members we have admitted in the past, if I erred in not following the lead of other clubs by allowing the system of 'black-balling'. It occurred to me, when I was drawing up the club's constitution, that if we allowed the other members to decide who was suitable to join the Diogenes, then we should soon find ourselves short of successful candidates. By their very nature, that our members should object to newcomers was a certainty. As a result, I felt any membership decisions should be in the hands of the committee. On days like this, I have cause to regret it.

"Did you fall, Sir Walpole?" I asked.

"What if I did?" he retorted. "The club has insurance. You can't expect me to pay for it."

As it happened, I was not expecting payment. I did, however, expect honesty. Sir Walpole was having none of it, and I am sorry to say he caused such a spectacle with his protestations that we quickly attracted the attention of a constable.

"What's going on here then?" said he.

"A minor disagreement amongst the members," I explained.

169

"Did the rioters do this?" he asked, nodding to the broken pot.

"No, Constable. It is a club matter. We will deal with it."

"As you wish, sir," said the constable. He paused and waggled his pencil at me. "I know you, don't I, sir? You were the fellow with the dog. Do you remember me? I'm Constable Robbins, sir."

Before I could answer, he had summoned his superior. A small man, barely an inch above the regulation height and with a thin, weasel-like face, came over with the hunched shoulders and disgruntled air of someone who has better things to do than be at the beck and call of the constabulary.

"Yes, Robbins, what is it?" said he.

"This is the gentleman I was telling you about, Inspector," said the constable. "He's related to that other fellow."

The inspector looked me up and down. "You sure about that, Robbins? He doesn't look much like Mr Holmes to me." Clearing his throat, he addressed me directly. "Am I right in understanding that you have a relation here in London?"

My thoughts naturally turned to Cousin Aubrey. The last I had heard of him, he had been arrested for mesmerising a policeman's horse outside Buckingham Palace. His defence was that he had a naturally soothing manner; the magistrate took a less tolerant view of the incident and fined him ten pounds.

"I have several," I replied. "Did you have someone particular in mind?"

"A consulting detective by the name of Mr Sherlock Holmes."

"He is my brother."

The little inspector scoffed. "Well, I never. I've always wondered if there were more like him at home, and now I know. You aren't a detective, are you, Mr Holmes?"

"Certainly not."

"Good, because it's bad enough with one of you interfering in our work without worrying about other members of the family too."

I must say that I took offence at this. "It seems to me that if you do not want his help, then you have only to say so."

He seemed taken aback. "I never said I needed his help, sir.

"Then perhaps you should tell him, Inspector Lestrade." He appeared even more shocked that I knew who he was. "Given the regularity with which your name appears in place of his, I should say that your criticism is unwarranted. Good day, sir."

I may have been a trifle brusque with the man, but one does not like to hear one's own brother criticised. That is a privilege I reserve for myself, and I consider myself better qualified for the task than random members of the public, especially those taking the credit at my brother's expense.

As for Sir Walpole Makepeace, I told him that his behaviour would be reported to the committee. If it had been my decision, I should have excluded him without further debate. Such is the inconvenience of having to rely on other people!

Friday, 9ᵗʰ December, 1887

The new office is far from satisfactory.

On the one hand, I have more space. On the other, I have too much space. One might call this contradictory, but there is something to be said for having just enough. One wonders if King Henry I had not gorged himself on a surfeit of lampreys but had taken a more moderate amount whether his reign would have staggered on for a few years more.

In my case, this surfeit of space has been playing on my mind to the exclusion of all else. My old furniture looks shabby in this pristine expanse and the old carpet is several feet too small on every side. My secretary tells me I appear somewhat 'lost' in my new surroundings, an epithet which should never be applied to a man of my position. If a man cannot find himself in his own office, then how can he be expected to perform adequately on the international scene?

The problem, then, with excess is that one is obliged to do something about it. I am told that I should acquire more furniture. Quantity is an issue. Too little and I shall appear miserly. Too much and we shall spend the next ten years forever falling over it.

There is also the question of the myriad of bookshelves, which my trusted legal volumes fail to fill. The office boy tells me – suddenly everyone is keen to offer advice, no matter how lowly – that I should buy some popular fiction, thus proving that I am 'informed as to the goings-on of the modern world'.

From what I have heard of popular fiction, it would appear to touch everything with the *exception* of the modern world. A mere glance at a stationer's window fills your sight with more nonsense written about the past and the future than a man needs to know. If one wishes to be informed about the 'modern world', as I told the boy, one should read the papers, and then with the consideration in mind that half of what the newspapers tell us is fabrication and the other half due to overheated imagination.

"Ah," said he, "but what about this new detective fellow I've been reading about? He's modern, sir. You should know about him."

"Is this a work of popular fiction?" I questioned him.

"It's in *Beeton's*," said he, taking a much-thumbed publication out of his pocket and leafing through the pages. "It says here he lives in Baker Street and his name's Mr Sherlock Holmes. 'Ere, he any relation of yours, sir?"

I maintained an admirable calm in light of this revelation. One does not like to appear taken aback before one's subordinates.

"Holmes is a common enough name," said I.

"Not that common," persisted the insolent fellow.

By now, several of the junior clerks were taking an interest.

173

"Cor, I'd be as pleased as Punch to have a detective in the family," said one.

"A *consulting* detective," I corrected him.

The office boy's eyes lit up. "Then you do know him!" he crowed. "Cos that's exactly what he says his profession is in 'ere."

"I most certainly do not," I returned, aware that I was reaching the limit of how many times I could in all good conscience deny my brother before emulating the example of St Peter. "As to how I know this fellow, it is my business to know things, young man."

"Even about this Mr Holmes?"

"I am full aware of Mr Sherlock Holmes's activities and the implications for this office. You would do well to remember that to the great mind, nothing is little."

"That's just what Mr Holmes says!" exclaimed the boy. "Are you sure you aren't related?"

I ended the conversation by giving the impudent lad one of my piercing glares. I have spent many years honing the technique to little avail on my brother, who endeavours to remain immune, so it is of some satisfaction to see that I have better success with ordinary mortals.

What did give me pause was my ignorance on the subject of this 'article'. I find I have to consult my journals as far back as 1881 to discover the first tentative mention of this literary enterprise on the part of Sherlock's fellow tenant. That the work has finally been completed and published comes as less of a surprise to me than the fact that I have not been informed. From this I can only conclude that it does not meet my brother's expectations – and by extension, mine – and therefore he has been unwilling to tell me of its existence lest I express my concern as to the contents.

Under these circumstances, the only course of action that remained to me was to acquire a copy of this wretched publication myself. I could not send the boy on my behalf, for that would awaken the suspicion of my subordinates. What it meant was my having to take a cab to one of the better booksellers in Marylebone, where my face was not known – I could hardly have gone to Mr Fishman, the usual supplier of my reading matter, who would delight in spreading the word that I had taken to reading less exulted material than *The Times* – and where I could be assured that a copy of the title would be in stock, having already made several frustrated stops along the way.

At the fifth attempt, at the bookshop of Garland and Luck, a few roads distant from my brother's now infamous domicile, the address of which was already on the lips of office boys and junior clerks alike, I found what I was looking for, a modest stock of *Beeton's Christmas Annual*.

If there exists a more unlikely introduction to what I have always been assured was a profession worthy of Sherlock's intelligence, then I have yet to find it. The cover was gaudy, in immoderate hues of red and yellow, with the bold headline, *A Study in Scarlet*, beneath which was an illustration of a young man applying a match to a lamp. What one had to do with the other was not immediately obvious. Only when I consulted the inside pages did I see my brother's name appearing regularly enough to confirm that this was the much-vaunted story.

Whilst thus engaged, another customer entered and was greeted by Mr Garland in the manner of an old friend. I should not have paid the fellow any heed, but for the sudden exclamation of his name by the shopkeeper.

"Why, Dr Watson," he enthused. "Good to see you, sir."

One assumes that there may be any number of Dr Watsons working in and around the capital. This close to Baker Street, however, and with a degree of familiarity with the shopkeeper beyond that of passing customer, I was led to the conclusion that this finally was the poor devil forced into sharing the rent on that tolerable pile with my brother.

Sherlock has maintained his reluctance to introduce us, on the grounds that when it comes to friends and family, never the twain should meet. I have respected this up to a point. One does not command the resources of Her Majesty's government without expecting some little service in return once in a while. A few discreet enquiries into the fellow's background confirmed that he was exactly as he purported to be, and was not as I had originally feared a wandering lunatic.

Certainly, seeing him for the first time now, he appeared to be in full possession of his wits. If, after six years of close personal contact with my brother, his constitution had not withered under the strain, then I suspected he would live to survive the ordeal. To describe him, I should say he was a well-made man of middle height, a little shorter than either Sherlock or myself, with a robust complexion and a neatly-trimmed moustache.

In manner, he was typical of the reformed medical man; that is to say, he did not give every member of the gathering a cursory glance to determine whether he was in the presence of a prospective patient. He was affable, pleasant and, to all intents and purposes, normal.

One hears about such people. Their occasional appearances give us reason for confidence that, unlike the dodo, they are not extinct. For Sherlock to have found such a specimen is extraordinary; for him to have retained the fellow's trust these past years was more so.

I admit to being intrigued, as one might be when encountering a rare and exotic bird on a jungle exploration. In that spirit, one should maintain one's calm, lest the prize be scared away. Mindful of Sherlock's injunction, I had determined to keep my distance and not introduce myself, but to observe from afar. Circumstance, however, conspires to break the firmest of resolves, and I soon found myself embroiled in a lamentable series of events not of my own making.

I had turned my back, lest he should see my face and suspect some familial resemblance, and pretended to read while the conversation between doctor and shopkeeper continued behind me. One does not like to eavesdrop, but sometimes it is unavoidable.

"A cold evening, Doctor," said Mr Garland.

"That is it. There is the promise of a fair lookout on the morrow. Did you see the sunset?"

"Ah, yes. 'Red sky at night, a sailor's delight', so they say. Now, what can I get you, sir? Your usual?"

"Yes, thank you, Mr Garland." There was a pause. "You still have your fine collection of *Beeton's*, I see."

"Oh, I've being selling one or two here and there. It will pick up, don't you worry. They'll all be gone by Christmas, you'll see."

"I hope so."

"Tell you what, Doctor, seeing as how you're here, would you consider signing a few? I can put a note up in the window – 'copies signed by the author himself'. Adds to the value, so it does. We'll shift a few more that way."

"Well, I don't know…"

That he was flattered by the remark was evident from his voice. Without having to look at the man, I could tell also that he was about to refuse, for his features had betrayed a turn for modesty that was inherent to his nature, a trait unknown in our family.

"People like a signed copy," Mr Garland persisted. "Take this gentleman here – now, you'd like a signed copy, wouldn't you, sir?"

It was suddenly borne upon me that I was the gentleman in question. Much to my chagrin I had been involved in this conversation and was in danger of making myself known to the one fellow in London I had sought to avoid. What I should have done was to leave the shop that instant. One does not wish to appear rude, however, nor discourage talent, so I mumbled something about the offer being a kind one and duly handed over my copy for the author's attention.

"To whom would you like me to dedicate it?" he asked.

"A general inscription, sir," I said, hurriedly.

He peered at me curiously. "Forgive me, have we met? I feel I should know you."

"No, sir, we have never had that pleasure."

If was brusque, I meant only to belay any turn of the conversation in the direction of my relations. He did not demur and a moment later I had in my hands a copy inscribed 'With Compliments, Dr John Watson'.

"You keep that safe," the shopkeeper advised me as I gave him the shilling for the publication. "Mark my words, that'll be worth a pretty penny in years to come[11]."

I took my leave with all due haste and retired to the Diogenes. Before a hearty fire and with a Scotch whisky by my side, I spent the better part of an hour reading a lurid tale of revenge and murder. No sooner had I set the thing aside than Sherlock appeared, bearing a large and, from the strained expression on his face, heavy bag. He dropped into the opposite armchair and with a contented sigh stretched out his legs to the fire.

It had been some weeks since I had seen him last, but from his manner, a casual observer would be led to the erroneous

---

[11] Mr Garland was correct. An original (unsigned) battered copy of *Beeton's Christmas Annual*, published November 1887, containing 'A Study in Scarlet', sold at auction with a hammer price of £15,500 in 2008.

178

conclusion that it had been a few days. There was no lengthy discussion as to my health or polite enquiry as to my activities. Like players in a game of chess, who have returned to the board after an absence, we simply pick up where we have left off, to use the vernacular. The length of time is unimportant; I daresay the distance of several years could separate our meetings and we would behave no differently towards each other. Possessing as we do the faculty for assessing at a glance how matters stand with the other, we are thus able to dispense with tedious pleasantries about the weather and the state of Great-Aunt Ada's bunions.

It sits well with us, although I daresay to others this behaviour may appear indifferent. On the contrary, with us, the opposite is true. Were our conversation to wander into those profitless avenues that preoccupy those obliged to humour distant relatives and work colleagues, we would consider ourselves very dull fellows indeed.

For my part, I did not need to ask what my brother had been doing. I could read that much from the state of his shoes and the mass of lumps and protrusions that marred the patterned surface of his carpet bag.

"Was it necessary to take yourself half across London in search of a bookseller?" I enquired. "Surely your local man would have sufficed?"

He regarded me passively. "The same could be said for you, Mycroft. Marylebone is a little out of your way."

"A great deal out of my way," I returned.

"You may lay the blame for that at my door," said Sherlock with a chuckle. "As of this evening, the only place in London you would be able to acquire a copy of *Beeton's* is at Messrs Garland and Luck."

"Why this omission?"

"Mr Garland knows me. Worse, he is an incurable gossip. I would not have it reach Watson's ears that I had purchased Mr Garland's entire stock of his debut novel."

"Extraordinary behaviour, Sherlock."

"Not at all. The only thing worse than sharing rooms with a consulting detective is sharing rooms with a new author. Sales have been slow and Watson has been fretting. It matters to him, you see."

"And by extension, it matters to you." I indicated my copy. "I have read it, Sherlock, despite your reluctance to inform me of its existence. I must admit to being somewhat perplexed by the attribution. Why doesn't he use his own name?"

"Watson expressed the concern that should he ever decide to take up practice, his literary efforts might jeopardise his success, lest he appear 'frivolous'. As he said himself, it isn't *The Lancet*. I do take his point, although I dispute whether the case was 'frivolous' in itself. What did you think of it?"

"I thought it... most inventive."

"Then you will understand that my concern is not for the story as such," said he. "Six years have passed. My credentials are established. I do not need my reputation bolstered in the eyes of the public. No, it is the principle of the thing. Granted, it is not how I would have done it, but I have been obliged to set my personal objections aside. Watson meant well, and it is incumbent upon me to respond in the same spirit."

"By buying all the outstanding copies in the London area? Well, brother, greater love hath no man than this, that he lay down his fortune for a friend."

My attempt at humour earned me a look cold enough to freeze the fires of Hell.

"That has nothing to do with it. I need calm if I am to work. Watson has nursed this novel of his with all the care one associates with an expectant parent. Now it has been published, he has taken to displaying all the symptoms of a new father. He visits our local bookseller every day and gives me regular reports as to how sales are progressing. I believe he fancies that failure on his part will reflect upon me, despite my reassurances to the contrary. I tell you, Mycroft, I may not be the most patient of men—"

I suppressed a laugh.

"—but I have endured much these past two weeks. Well, it shall be no longer. Watson shall go forth tomorrow to discover that the populace have taken him to their hearts and turned out in droves to acquire a copy of his first work!"

He gave me a look of triumph, although whether at having taken his own initiative in the matter or for the anticipated reaction of the fragile author I could not say.

"A pity you deigned to buy only the one copy from Mr Garland," he went on. "I shall have to send an associate to purchase the remaining copies. I wish you had told me of your intention, Mycroft."

"I was only made aware of it today through a chance remark by a member of my staff. Nor would my informing you have made the slightest difference. I could not have followed your course because the author was present at the time of my purchase."

Sherlock sat bolt upright in his chair. "You met Watson?"

That I still on occasion possess the faculty for provoking such a reaction in my brother is a source of some secret pride to me. A man should always keep something in reserve, especially against a sibling who has made observation and deduction the means of making a living.

"I did."

"What did you say to him?"

"Little that would be of interest to you, Sherlock. I did not identify myself. Your secret is safe. You may rest your mind on that point."

181

He relaxed back into his chair, something like relief twitching at his features.

I daresay any other man may have taken offence at such a reaction. I am not, however, any other man. I understand more than Sherlock might allow. Family is thrust upon us, like gout and taxes. Friends, like greatness, have to be earned. Thus they are all the more valuable for it and demand the closest of care.

"Now you have met," said he, after a long minute, "I suppose a formal introduction would not be out of the question."

"From what I saw of him, I believe he could stand the shock."

Sherlock smiled. "I should say he would be intrigued and delighted. I fancy he believes me to be an orphan."

"You are. Our parents are dead. That you have a brother does not change that fact."

"Well, as you say, I shall have to engineer a meeting."

"Is he a club man? Bring him here."

"Heavens, no. Watson is gregarious by nature. The thought of shunning his fellow man would be unthinkable."

"Poor devil. We all have our burdens. Well, it is a pity. Are you staying, by the way? I understand trout is on the menu tonight."

He accepted my invitation, which left only the problem of the quantity of books at his feet. What was he to do with them, he wanted to know. He could hardly take them home with him. Dr Watson would likely stumble across them and demand an explanation.

Which is how I have become the unwilling and unhappy owner of a collection of some five hundred copies of *Beeton's*. Her Majesty's government moves in mysterious ways, but not I fear in the question of disposing of debut novels. I shall have to hire a man to take them away. What becomes of them after that is not my concern.

Let them be consigned to a watery grave at the bottom of the Thames for all I care. As long as a certain doctor never finds out, I daresay it does not matter one jot.[12]

---

[12] We may speculate as to whether this is the reason why original copies are so rare today.

Wednesday, 26 June, 1888

Mr Melas, who lodges on the floor above mine, is a quiet, well-mannered man, an interpreter and guide by profession, and sensible in thought, word and deed. So when he came to me yesterday morning in great distress of mind, babbling about a man with sticking plaster over his face, my first inclination was to believe the poor fellow when he told me he had been the victim of an unusual and disturbing experience[13].

My next thought, as I listened to his tale, was that this sort of business was much more in Sherlock's line of interest than mine.

Today, therefore, having exhausted the limit of my involvement in the case, I sent a wire to my brother inviting him to join me at the Diogenes. That he would come was a foregone

---

[13]A grease patch obscuring the date and the paucity of entries before and after this entry means that the date of the story, *The Greek Interpreter*, is still unknown.

conclusion, for I keep my summons short and stripped of detail these days, thus ensuring his attendance if only to discover what mystery lies behind my words. What I did not know was whether he would come alone, for despite much talk and many promises after my accidental meeting with Dr Watson last December, Sherlock has remained unforthcoming on the subject of a formal introduction.

Having baited my hook, I cast my line and waited for results. After tea, as the clock was chiming the half hour, the lure proved irresistible and my brother duly appeared at the door of my private study.

"Come in, dear boy, come in," I urged him.

"I would rather you came out," said he. "There's someone I would like you to meet in the Strangers' Room."

"Well, well," said I. "How true was the Bard when he remarked *'how wretched is the poor man that hangs on princes' favours'*. To what do I owe this honour?"

"The promise of something a little out of the ordinary. You do not issue invitations lightly, Mycroft. That deserved some reward in return."

"In other words, you would not have come if you had not sensed I had an ulterior motive."

"Quite so. By the way, I did not mention your wire to Watson, and I would rather you did not either. He believes this visit arose naturally from the turn of our discussion."

"Better that he does not realise he has been brought here under false pretences, you mean. Very well, brother. If that is how it must be."

"I insist."

"Any other conditions?" I enquired.

He considered. "Try to restrain your natural inclination to embarrass me."

I did, of course, try to keep to the spirit of that latter stricture, although without much success. Embarrassing my brother is one of the few pleasures left to me in life, along with Mrs Tully's beefsteak pies. I had in mind, however, that we were in the presence of a 'susceptible', that is to say an author, one whose brain seeks to convert every new experience into the banality of the written word.

I daresay I was affable enough. I shook the fellow's hand, made mention of his literary efforts as a chronicler of my brother's doings and sought to show that he had not entirely usurped my position as confidante by making a vague allusion to a trifling affair Sherlock had been worrying his brains over the week before.

It felt fitting too that we resurrect our old game of observation and deduction, if only to disprove any slanders my brother had spread about my slothful and idle demeanour. I triumphed, naturally, owing to a failure on Sherlock's part to draw the necessary inferences from certain articles in our observed gentleman's possession. To me, they were as clear as day, and I do wonder if the time has come for Sherlock to consider whether a pair of spectacles is not in order to correct this weakness. Certainly I shall have to mention it to him when next we are alone.

If I dozed whilst Mr Melas told his tale, it was not through lack of interest on my part, but due to over-familiarity with the details. Having heard it once and acted on what little information I was able to glean, listening to a retelling of the events, complete this time with a fair imitation of the voices of the various characters – including half-decent womanly tones that fairly jolted me from my slumbers in the fear that a female had penetrated the club's formidable defences – was liable to pall. Sherlock was intrigued, however, and I read the same attentiveness in the eyes of his companion.

186

I would say it was an unbecoming quality in a medical man, except that Dr Watson appears to have avoided the morbid strain that besets his profession when encountering a rare and exotic disease by treating it as an isolated phenomenon, set apart from the poor devil in its grip. That is to say, Watson displayed what I can only describe as a certain sympathy for the unfortunates in this drama.

It really was a most remarkable thing. Set against the reaction of my brother, the contrast between the two was all the more marked. Pity for one's fellow man is no doubt admirable, but can only serve to muddy the facts. In my opinion, it is also misplaced. Finer feelings, like tender hearts, are liable to be trampled, or mistaken for weakness, which is worse. Similarly, becoming misty-eyed over the mention of a fair maid suggests maudlin tendencies that are liable to manifest themselves in idealism of the worst kind, as anyone who has had the misfortune to read a novel of 'romance' can readily testify.

I daresay no room in London at that time held two fellows who differed in personality as much as Sherlock and Dr Watson. Knowing how they got together, I can only wonder at how they have *remained* together. Fire and ice have ever been natural enemies, and yet one without the other is devoid of purpose. So it is with people, one supposes.

These musings of mine, allied with a fortuitous turn of good fortune, I fear subsequently led me to commit a liberty that I had hitherto avoided. A letter from a Mr J Davenport directly pertaining to the case gave me the excuse I needed and so I took a cab to Baker Street, passing my brother and the good doctor in the street along the way. I had some slight trouble with Sherlock's landlady, a redoubtable woman, diminutive in height and gargantuan in determination, in convincing her as to my honourable intentions.

187

"The brother of Mr Holmes?" said she, her voice dripping with doubt and accusation. "You don't look anything like him."

"I assure you I am, my good woman."

"Don't you 'good woman' me," she retorted. "Mr Holmes has warned me about the likes of you. I've had all sorts coming knocking at my door at all hours of the day and night, trying to gain admittance to Mr Holmes's quarters, and they've all called me 'my good woman'. The next thing you'll be doing is giving me a shilling for my trouble. Well, it won't do!"

I dropped the coin back into my pocket and instead took out my card.

"'Mr Mycroft Holmes'," she read out, in tones that lacked enthusiasm or conviction. "You could have got that from anywhere. You might have had it printed up especially for the occasion."

"My dear lady," I said, careful this time to avoid the alternative, "it seems to me that the only way I can convince you is by practical test. Speaking as one who has the misfortune to share lodgings with my brother in the past and is resolved never again to repeat the exercise, I trust you will recognise my sincerity when I say, from regrettable experience, that he is quite the worst tenant in London!"

This gained me immediate entry.

In Sherlock's absence, I investigated this hallowed domain of his. It was much as I had expected. A trail of assorted clutter led me to his bedroom, with its unusual criminal decoration, lurid books and scattered clothes. How anyone could live in such a way is beyond me. And yet, outside of these walls, he appears as immaculate a gentleman as one would expect to meet in the dappled, tree-lined streets in Kensington or grey-clad Westminster.

One may speculate as to which is the real and which the assumed image. The thought occurs that my brother's inclination

188

may tend towards idling about the place in his dressing gown, tossing shag over the carpet and spearing his correspondence to the mantelpiece with a jack knife.

If so, I cannot blame him. I have found more contentment in my club with my slippers on my feet and none for company but the crackling of the fire on a cold winter's night than all the meetings over tea and biscuits with the Prime Minister. I believe if more people were honest about their likes and wants, then the restaurants would stand deserted and the sales of pipes and carpet slippers would quadruple overnight.

But – alas! – are we not all compelled to observe etiquette and partake in this grand charade? How fortunate the man who can truly claim to be his own master.

In the present instance, I found a seat amidst the clutter and helped myself to one of Sherlock's cigars, unimaginatively hidden in the coal scuttle, whilst I waited for his return. Eventually, I was alerted to his impending arrival by a brisk step on the stair. I believe my presence was something of a surprise, if his expression was anything by which to judge, and I made some vague excuse about an interest in the case as reason for my being there. Then I produced the letter from Mr Davenport and gave the pair the benefit of my deductions.

I was all for driving over to the fellow's lodgings in Brixton, but Sherlock took a different view of the matter. So it was that we ended the evening at The Myrtles, Beckenham, fortuitously for Mr Melas, but less so for Mr Kratides, who, despite the doctor's attentions, was more in need of a priest than a physician. Our birds, Latimer and Kemp had flown, which cast a downcast note on the proceedings, although I daresay retribution will find them in due course. A few words in certain ears may speed the natural course of justice to a satisfactory conclusion.

For my part, I am pleased to be able to report that I disported myself with some distinction throughout. Indeed, I showed an exceptional turn of energy that left me quite liverish by the time we were homeward bound. No doubt one day I shall have the pleasure of reading an account of the affair in some published edition of Sherlock's cases. Dr Watson hinted as much during the course of our journey. Whether I am given my fair due remains to be seen.

However, if I have gleaned anything from this experience, it is that I begin to see what Sherlock sees in this chosen profession of his. Admittedly, there is not a great deal to choose between government and detective work. We solve problems, albeit on lesser and greater scales. Finding solutions to the apparently insolvable is at the heart of what we do – which brings me to the problem of Dr Watson.

It cannot end well, this alliance, but one day it surely must. Dr Watson is what I should call 'a marrying man', and it cannot be long before his days as a bachelor are brought to a close by a pretty smile and winning ways. That it should occur in the course of one of these escapades of theirs is perhaps inevitable, but to my mind it would be better if it occurred independently of that association. How Sherlock would react to his practice becoming a marriage bureau I do not care to speculate.

I had not fully appreciated the situation until I had a chance to observe them over the course of this case. They are as giddy as schoolboys and twice as boisterous. It is equally obvious that the doctor considers my brother a 'friend'. I wonder how much it is reciprocated on Sherlock's part. Superficial it may appear, but I seem to remember his efforts December last to appease the new author and the resulting tide of *Beeton's Christmas Annuals* that tested the limit of my seasonal goodwill.

As I say, it cannot end well. Far better, however, that it comes at the hands of a woman than one of the criminal fraternity.

But perhaps I have spent too long in Whitehall's brown corridors, as Sherlock is wont to remind me, and I have grown old and suspicious. The unlikeliest dwelling may endure above other structures when the foundations are strong and the walls proof against shocks. So it may be in this case.

Well, time will tell and these journals shall record. I can only trust that in either case, it does not disturb my routine too much. After all, being the brother of London's only consulting detective is already wearisome enough!

Acknowledgements

It was my grandfather who inspired my interest in Sherlock Holmes. A great devotee himself, he knew the stories by heart and the details inside and out. Long before I ever learned of Sherlockian scholarship or pastiches, we were busy making our own theories about Reichenbach and formulating our own explanations for Watson's wandering wounds. Our starting point was always and only the stories, and I have been a canon purist ever since.

In a long list of acknowledgements, first and foremost must be the thanks I owe to my mother, Frances, without whose endless support, patience and encouragement this book would not have been possible.

My gratitude also to Marguerite, an indefatigable proof-reader and good friend.

Thanks also must go to the readers and writers of the online archive where I first experimented with my writings. You are the best of friends, and the best of critics.

I also have to thank Derrick Belanger for encouraging me to make the leap from internet to print. It has been a challenge, but very rewarding.

And finally, my thanks go to Sir Arthur Conan Doyle for the creation of memorable characters and the greatest detective the world has ever known. Long may his adventures continue!

Best wishes to all,
S.F. Bennett

Belanger Books

25755578R00116

Printed in Great Britain
by Amazon